MYSTICAL

The

Return

A book by

BENJAMIN A JOSEPH

MYSTICAL

The

Return

This book is a total work of fiction, based entirely on author's imagination. All characters, names, action place and all others reference are imaginary or manipulation. Any resemblances are accidental, as the author had no one or place in mind at the time of writing.

In Loving Memory of Late Mr. Joseph

My DAD

Terser

"Slim! Slim!!" she yells in fright as she runs toward the entrance of the house. "Those boys are faceless," she screams in fear as she opens the door and enters.

Inside the living room, the atmosphere is eerily calm. This scares her even more; the house is quiet and cold, with no aroma of food that had earlier filled the room. The table looks as if it hasn't been used for a long time.

"Slim!" she manages to mutter under her breath, fear etched across her face.

Then she sees him coming down the stairs. She runs to him and hugs him tightly.

CONTENT

Chapter One

The Burial

The proceedings were led by the vicar of the family's new church, followed by a group of young men who handled the coffin with great care. The family walked behind them, escorted by a few sympathizers, as they had not been long in the community.

An owl hooted in the distance, sending chills down the spines of most sympathizers, but they continued walking at a steady pace with the bereaved family. It was nighttime, and Mrs. Miguel had wished to give her only son a warm burial in the morning, but the doctor, a close family friend, had advised against it. He explained that the body was greatly damaged, with some parts already beginning to rot, and any attempt to sew it up had proven futile. "Given his age, he really had delicate skin, and putting him in the morgue or embalming him won't do much good," he had said, fearing the odor the body could cause in the morgue.

The undertakers waited patiently at the spot they had dug, where the body would finally be laid to rest. The cemetery was an old one, used by the church to lay to rest the bodies of departed brethren. It was old, cold, and silhouetted, as that was all the church could afford, even for this middle-aged young fellow. His mother, a devoted Christian, believed that burying her son in a godly house would ensure his peace in the next world.

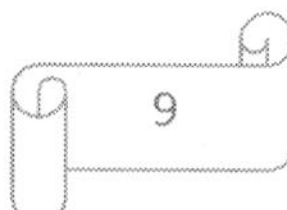

The coffin was lowered by the young men, none of whom he had known while he was alive. Pastor Antonio Harden stepped forward to lead the farewell prayer for the deceased. He had known him since his childhood and had also conducted his father's funeral a long time ago. However, he had never foreseen this coming. The undertakers had done a good job cleaning and dressing him in his best suit. He looked handsome even in the coffin, as if he were only sleeping and would wake up any moment.

The pastor felt a loop of tears welling up in his eyes; he summoned his courage, as he could not afford to grieve in front of the family now. He wiped off the tears and walked to give his farewell sermon. An owl hooted again, but the bereaved mother and her daughter did not hear or notice it.

"We are here to give a farewell service to our beloved brother and son..." he began, pausing to clear his throat before continuing. "Nickerson Miguel Eglin was like a son to me... Sincerely, 'like' would be an understatement. He is a son I wish I had. He was with us just this morning, but now he rests in the bosom of our Heavenly Father. We have no right to question what God does; otherwise, I would have asked him a million questions right away. But as we all know, whatever He does is perfect. God gives and God takes."

He stopped, raising his head to observe the youths who had come to the funeral and to console the family. "My advice to you, fellow brethren, is that you live your life as if every day were the last..." He paused again before continuing. "We pray that God will console the family of the bereaved, and my prayer is that your soul finds peace in your new abode, Nickerson Miguel Eglin, as we put you to rest here on earth. Dust to dust and ash to ash. Farewell, our beloved son and brother. Farewell, Nickerson."

"Amen!" the sympathizers echoed. At a signal, the undertakers began lowering the coffin into the earth below.

Mrs. Miguel watched the last of her son as he was laid to rest. She remembered the saying that it was normal for a son to bury his old folks, but an abomination for the old folks to bury their children. She gazed at his face as it was lowered into the earth; it looked bright as if he were smiling at her. It all seemed like an evil nightmare to her. She remembered just that morning, how he had taken his bath and dressed up in his black suit. She had told him to hurry up as the plane would be leaving by 10 a.m. "But you must eat your food first," she had said. "I made it myself."

"Oh, Mom, you're just so caring. I don't know what I would do without you," he had complimented.

"Well, thank your sister too. She helped as well," she had replied.

Mayan had walked to the dining table holding a cup of coffee, sipping it as she watched him eat the varieties their mother had made for him. Chicken, fresh meat, and a plate of pasta accompanied by wine juice—those were really too much for breakfast, but they were used to this tradition. Their mother always did that whenever any of her children traveled.

She sat on one of the chairs, watching him quietly as he ate the food carefully in his usual slow manner.

He stared at her for a moment. "What is it? Why are you inspecting me?" he had asked. Mayan, who was just twenty and almost done with medical school, sat still. "Aren't you going to say something? You bore me, you know?" he teased her.

"You better be careful before you stain your white," she replied coldly, still sipping her tea.

He inspected his shirt briefly; it was still clean and well-ironed. He dropped his knife and fork on the table, stretched out his hands, and called to her. "Help me get this suit off me," he said. She stood up, walked up to him, and carefully helped him remove the suit, hanging it on the back of the seat he was sitting on. He picked up an apron and hung it around his neck. "Thanks, little sister," he said.

Just then, their mother joined. "How was the food, my prince?" she asked.

"Mom, it was very delicious. I can swear it was the best I have had so far," he flattered.

"That is what you always say," Mayan retorted.

"Well, I am being serious now. I wish you could cook as well as mom," he teased again, fond of teasing her.

"She is good," Mrs. Miguel interrupted. "Besides, she is twenty and will soon get married. However, not until she completes medical school!" she said emphatically.

"Seriously, she is twenty?" he asked.

"Of course, she turned twenty last month," Mrs. Miguel replied. "Do you take her for a baby?" she asked.

"No, Mom, I really thought she was like thirty. She looks even older than me. Can't you see that, Mom?"

Mayan had the mug to her mouth and almost spilled out the contents in reaction to his joke. She held out her teacup and would have thrown it at him if not for their mother's intervention.

"Hold it right there, Mayan! Can't you see he's already dressed up? Unless you want him to miss his flight, you know he sucks at dressing," Mrs. Miguel pointed out.

She held back the cup and grinned at him. "You are lucky Mom saved you this time. You would have worn a stained shirt to Los Angeles, and that way, I'm sure they would have hurriedly given you the approval for your law firm," she said jokingly.

Nick studied her for a brief moment and laughed at her reaction to his joke. "I'm sure you will be the last person on earth who would want to see me travel in a messed-up shirt," he said. "But seriously, I love the way my joke got you."

"Get up and start going," his mother hurried him. "It's getting late already." He helped himself to a piece of chicken, chewing it while simultaneously cleaning his hands with a piece of tissue paper, then rising to his feet to go.

"Let me help you with your suit!" Mayan offered, standing and helping him put the suit back on.

"Okay, I'm all set now!" he said. "Thanks, little sister. I will see you soon. Mom!" he called out. "I'm on my way," he added as the driver appeared. Mrs. Miguel was out again.

"Have you picked every necessary document?" she asked. "You know the U.S. to Mexico isn't far."

"Sure, Mama. I did all that last night," he said.

"Hurry up now. You can't afford to miss the flight. And please drive carefully, Mr. Igor..."

"Never mind, Mama," he said, interrupting her. "I will do the driving. I'm sure that way, your mind will be at peace. Is that ok, Mama?"

She nodded with a smile in reply to his suggestion. "Well, thanks a bunch. I will see you soon. I love you, Mom," he added as he hopped into the big Ford jeep, with the driver sitting in the passenger front seat beside him. His sister handed him his briefcase.

"Thanks again, Mayan. I don't know what I will do without you guys," he said, stopping abruptly and staring at her briefly. "I've got something to tell you and Mother, but I guess that will wait till I get back." He ignited the car and drove out of his family mansion.

** ** **

Mayan and her mother had waited five hours for the driver's return or a call from him, but nothing happened until 4:00 PM that evening.

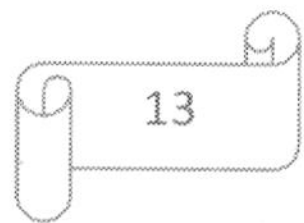

The phone rang at 4:00 PM, and Mayan jumped to her feet in excitement. "Maybe he has gotten there already," she exclaimed as she walked up to the phone and picked up the receiver. "Mrs. Miguel's mansion," she said. "You are speaking with Mayan, her daughter."

"Yes, I know," the caller retorted sharply. "Is Elizabeth around?"

Her hand clung to the receiver tightly, and perspiration ran down her face. She recognized Dr. Greg's voice; he was one of their family's close friends. He and their mother used to work together at the hospital before she decided to quit her medical career and dedicate her life to helping her children after the death of her late husband, Mr. Miguel. He had also been her mentor and had been given her some basic training in the hospital. However, today she was absent, and she knew he was not calling for that.

"Yes, Mom is around," she replied, pausing for a moment. "Should I give her the phone?" she asked.

"No, never mind," he replied after a brief hesitation. "Just tell her that the two of you should come to the hospital now," he said emphatically and hung up.

Mayan felt a thud in her heart, now she is more convinced of her earlier hunch. "Who was it?" Mrs. Miguel asked. "And why do you suddenly look pale?"

"It was Dr. Greg," she said. "And he asked that we come to the hospital right away."

Mrs. Miguel stood still. She had been a medical practitioner for quite some time and knew the effect of the call. "What did he say happened?" she asked curiously.

"Let's stop wasting time, Mom," Mayan retorted sharply. "Let's hurry up and go now."

They rushed to the old blue Cadillac, and Mayan drove with her hands uneasy at the wheel. Some minutes later, they arrived at the hospital, and a nurse showed them to the doctor's office.

Dr. Greg stood up and walked towards them to receive his old colleague. "You are welcome, Betty," he said.

"What happened to my son?" she asked firmly, interrupting him before he could finish speaking.

He paused and observed her for a moment. "You have to calm down, Elizabeth," he said.

"Is he dead?" she asked anxiously, her voice unsteady.

"No, he is not dead! But let's just hope for a miracle," he managed to reply. "Let's go see him right away," he added, his voice sounding a little choky, which didn't sound good to both Mayan and her mother.

Hand in hand, mother and daughter walked after the doctor. They reached a ward, and the doctor took them inside. A man lay on a bed, badly injured, and he was given oxygen support. A nurse stood close, observing him.

"How is he doing?" Dr. Greg asked the nurse.

"He is responding, sir, but I guess it is going to take a long time to recover," she replied.

Mayan and her mother recognized the man at once. It was Mr. Igor, their driver.

"What happened to them?" Mayan asked anxiously. "And where is my brother? Is he dead?"

"Calm down, Mayan. You just have to calm down, and let's just hope for a miracle," he said as he walked them to an emergency ward. "Mr. Igor was really fortunate he wasn't driving," he explained and paused. "A speeding car took a wrong turn in front of them at the T junction close to the airport road. Nick was quick to hit the brake, but unfortunately, a truck was coming at a vicious speed. It hit them brutally," he said, pausing with a grimace. "They were brought here since morning, and I have been doing all I could, especially for Nick, so I thought I should call you," he concluded as they entered the emergency room.

They entered the ward. It was a private emergency ward with a bed in the middle by the wall. Nick lay motionless on it, the monitor beeping faintly, and an oxygen machine was used to support his breathing.

Mrs. Miguel walked closer to the spot where he lay and regarded him briefly. This wasn't the same boy she had nurtured that morning. His head was badly stitched, and it seemed the doctor had done everything in his power to put it in this form. He was bandaged everywhere, looking weak, pale, and helpless, and she didn't need to be told that he wouldn't make it.

She walked up to him and held his hand, kneeling by the edge of the bed, and wept over his still body. Mayan also did the same, holding his other hand and weeping as well. The thought of losing her only brother was just too big a blow she couldn't handle.

"Oh! My son," she said while weeping bitterly. "Why must you go this early? I wish I could turn back the hands of time; I would have given anything just to take your place. I would have driven you myself. Perhaps I would have taken your place," she said while still weeping and lamenting.

They remained like that for over three hours, with the monitor now beeping more faintly.

At 7:00 PM, the doctor tapped Mrs. Miguel's shoulder and asked to speak with her. She followed him to a corner of the ward, looking pale and fragile. He noticed how the tragic news had broken her, especially as she now knew that he had little chance of surviving the accident.

"Hmm," Doctor Greg said, then cleared his throat. "I guess you know as much as I do that he can't make it. Though the monitor can keep beeping forever, his body is just too weak to help his heart. I would suggest we unplug the machine and relieve him of…"

"No, I won't allow you!" she interrupted him firmly. "I will not do that to my son. It's like killing him myself. I know he is badly damaged and it will take more than just a miracle for him to survive this. However, I will let him depart peacefully. Besides, my son never sleeps without saying goodnight to me. Let's wait, perhaps there could be a miracle."

Dr. Greg almost laughed at her confidence but controlled himself. "Mrs. Miguel, I really respect you a lot, and I know the situation here is really critical. However, we have to be rational. Now let's assume he woke up, which I don't see as a possibility, and I'm quite sure you are aware of that as well. Besides, what is the guarantee that he will not be mentally unstable? Though I'm not against you wanting him to go peacefully, him waking up will take more than just a miracle. Besides, I would advise he be buried tonight because his skin is badly damaged."

"I won't discuss that now!" she retorted firmly, grimacing at him. "At least he is not dead yet." She walked back to his bed with Mayan still clinging to his hand as if it would transfer life to him. She sat by his side too, bracing herself for the worst.

At 8:00 PM, something extraordinary happened. The monitor began to beep normally, and Dr. Greg walked closer to observe it, surprised at what was happening. Mrs. Miguel and Mayan stood to their feet as Nick opened his eyes, though he looked pale and weak.

"Nick!!" Mayan exclaimed with joy on her face. His mother held his hands tightly. He signaled with his eyes to them; Mrs. Miguel, Mayan, and Dr. Greg understood what he meant. Dr. Greg shook his head in disagreement, but Mrs. Miguel nodded in approval.

The doctor walked up to him and removed the oxygen support, and he breathed out heavily. "Mum," he said with a voice that sounded so faint and hardly audible, "I'm so...rry."

"Baby, I'm here now," Mrs. Miguel replied while still holding his hand firmly. "Relax so you can gain some strength," she advised. He shook his head at her and tried to force a smile.

"Ma..Ya..n!" he called to his sister, who sat by the edge of his bed, using her hand to caress his hair. "Ta..ke c..ar.e of m..um," he said..

"Please stop saying that!" she said with tears in her eyes. "You will be strong again, and you can go on teasing me as much as you want. I swear I won't get mad at you again, but please don't leave us just yet…" she pleaded.

"Mu.m, please do what the doc..tor asked you to," he stuttered. "He h..as tried his best. And pro..mise me you will accept her if she co..mes," he pleaded.

"I will. I promise, I will," Mrs. Miguel said, even though she had no clue about whom he was referring to. She felt obliged to accept all his last wishes.

"Ma..yan, I lo..ve you. Plea..se ta..ke care of m.a..ma…." he said, and the ventilator monitor began to beat faster. Doctor Greg rushed to replace the oxygen support, but it did no good as everything went silent again.

He checked his pulse, and it was cold. He raised his head at Mrs. Miguel. Mayan understood the gesture, and cold tears began dropping from her eyes; she wished she could bring him back.

"Let him rest, doctor. Let him rest," Mrs. Miguel finally said.

That was the last moment of her son with them, and all that happened just today. She looked at the coffin as it was finally lowered into the earth. "Farewell, Nick. Farewell, my beloved son," she said, wiping the tears from her face.

Chapter Two

Somewhere in Santa Clara, Cuba

A taxi parked at the west end. Slim, as he was popularly known here, arrived in Santa Clara at 14:00. Mrs. Montez and her two boys were outside playing a card game when they were the first to welcome him back. They wondered why his friend Cruz had not informed them and why he didn't go to pick him up from the airport as usual.

She and her kids ran to him. "Welcome, Slim! How was your trip? We never knew you were coming this soon," she said, pausing to scrutinize him for a moment. "And how strange of you! I'm so sure you didn't inform your friend of your coming either?" Mrs. Montez asked curiously.

Slim gave her his usual charming smile and hugged her. "I wanted to surprise everyone this time," he said. "Well! How are you doing? And how come I didn't see the girls?" he asked.

"Same reason why I'm asking you why you didn't inform your friend," she replied. "The girls have moved to the school boarding house. They want to concentrate on their studies, and I'm sure your house must be in a mess; you know the boys are no good at cleaning," she added.

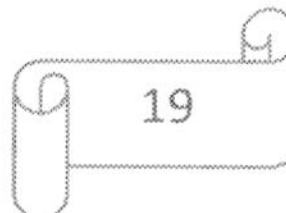

Slim grinned, then smiled at her. "Never mind, Mrs. Montez. They will do…." He said, and hesitates briefly, "So Anna and Clara have now decided to go to the school boarding house?" he asked while still smiling. "Well, that sounds good…. I'm sure now the boys will learn to give you a hand with the house chores," he added observantly.

"Well, I've got to go now," Mrs. Montez said. "I have to do some shopping before it gets late. We have no groceries at the moment…. However, it's nice seeing you again, Slim. I will come to check on your progress when I return."

"Thanks, Mrs. Montez. It's nice seeing you too," he replied, turning to the boys. "Ok boys, let's go in; we've got some cleaning to do."

Jerald, the eldest, grabbed his luggage and was trying to take it in all by himself. Alex, the youngest and last son of Mrs. Montez, struggled with the bag with him, knowing Slim usually had gifts for them whenever he came back.

"Hold it, boys! Handle the luggage carefully; there are a lot of gifts for you all in there," he said. Alex, at his word, smiled and left the luggage for his brother to carry.

Jerald, who was just ten years of age, and Alex, just eight, always came around to play at his place whenever he was around. "So Slim, how is Brazil? You never got to tell us last time," Jerald asked curiously.

"Yep," he replied. "And that was bad of me, I guess. But I'm back now, and we've got a lot of time together…. I promise you guys are going to get tired of listening to me," he joked.

They arrived at his living room; it looked really messy and untidy.

"We've got a lot of work here, boys. So which of you is going to handle this?" he asked.

"I, please!" the two boys echoed, pleading with him.

Slim laughed at them for a moment. "Well, let's go upstairs. I believe there is much work up there, so I guess we finish up there, then come back here and do it all together. Is that ok with you guys?" he asked.

The boys nodded in agreement. They got to his room upstairs, and for some reason, it wasn't as untidy as downstairs.

"Ok boys, let's relax a little; later we'll do the cleaning," he suggested, and they sat on the center rug in his bedroom.

The house was a two-bedroom self-contained bungalow, with two bedrooms and a restroom upstairs, and the kitchen, living room, store, and garage on the ground floor. The house was surrounded by a hedge of flowers, and at the back, there was a small garden he made for himself. The second room was seldom used; it was for his sister whenever she came around to spend her holidays here.

The house was surrounded by a short fence with a long lane from the front gate to the garage, which was attached to the house and also had a parking space. The house was opposite Mrs. Montez's.

The boys sat on the tiger rug in his room, and he drew the luggage closer and sat opposite the boys, facing them.

"So what have you boys been doing all this while I traveled?" he asked.

"We have been doing nothing!" Alex said emphatically. He was the youngest and most talkative.

Slim laughed at him. "You can't be doing nothing," he said. "You mean you have not been helping your mom?" he asked.

"Never mind him," Jerald retorted angrily. "He has been eating all the food at home," he added sarcastically. "And do you know your friend Israel has been coming here often? He would have taken your wife if Mom had not sent them to the boarding house," he added.

Slim laughed at his joke. He knew Mrs. Montez usually teased Anna by calling her his wife. "So Israel is dating Anna now?" he asked, pausing briefly. "Well, let him have her," he said jokingly. He brought out the picture of the girl he was dating and showed it to them.

"Wow! Slim! Who is she?" the boys asked with curiosity.

"She is Estella, my future wife," he said.

"Wow! She's really cute," the boys echoed, admiring the picture even at their tender age. "When is she coming here?" Alex asked.

"Maybe she might come, or maybe she might not," Slim replied. "But let's not talk about that now, ok?" The boys nodded in agreement. "Now let me give you your gifts."

He opened the luggage and brought out a mini laptop, which he gave to Jerald. "This is a game laptop, and it plays all kinds of PlayStation games. I only hope you will take good care of it," he said.

Jerald ran around the room in excitement. This was his first time having his own personal PlayStation game, and in the form of a laptop. Alex ran after him, trying to collect it. "Here is yours, Alex, unless you want me to keep it for myself," Slim said.

At his words, Alex came back, and Slim gave him two packages. One was an electric remote-control car, and the other a portable PlayStation 3 game.

"Wow! This is awesome," Alex exclaimed with joy. Jerald came back to examine Alex's gift, feeling a little jealous but happy with his own gift too.

They were still screaming when Mrs. Montez came in. "And what was the noise all about?" she asked angrily. She was upset, especially at the state of the house. "Oh my God! You guys haven't done anything here since I left," she observed angrily, gazing at the messy state of the house, and most especially angry at Slim for not making the boys clean up the mess. It was already evening, and she had to go prepare dinner. She stopped suddenly as the boys showed her the expensive gifts Slim had brought them.

"Oh my God, Slim! This is excessively much; it must have cost you a fortune. And look at them! They have not even lifted a finger to help you clean up the house."

"Never mind, Mrs. Montez. I will do that later. It's just that I'm so happy seeing them again," he admitted.

"I am really happy about the gifts," she said. "I hope you came with mine as well?" she asked jokingly. "But seriously, I'm disappointed at the mess. I guess I just have to go finish up with the cooking and come back up here to help."

"That will be kind of you, Mrs. Montez, but I think it won't really be necessary. I really want to get some rest now. It's been a long day, and I'm so tired after the trip. I just need to rest my weary head, and maybe when I wake up, I will do the cleaning," he said.

She grimaced and then laughed at him. "You want to sleep? Your bed is messy. I don't see how you will sleep on it that way," she noted.

"No, it's not," Slim retorted. "I made it already."

Mrs. Montez laughed and turned to look at the big-sized bed, and her laugh ceased halfway. She knew what she had seen when she had come in, and it was not even up to two minutes ago. Besides, she never saw him leave the spot where she had met them. It would take five minutes to make the huge-sized bed, not to mention cleaning the messy state she had seen it in when she came in. However, now it all looked tidy and really cleaned up in the blink of an eye. She wondered how it happened; only magic could have done that.

She stood amazed for a brief moment, wondering what had just happened. "Yep, you have cleaned it," she finally said, still wondering what mystic event had taken place here. She knew what she had seen, and she was sure the bed was untidy when she came in, and all that in less than a few minutes.

"Boys!" she called calmly. "Let's get going. Slim needs to rest. We will come back tomorrow to help with the cleaning. And I hope you have thanked Slim for the gifts?"

"Thanks, Slim," the boys echoed. They made to leave, and Mrs. Montez stopped at the door.

"You can come to have dinner with us when you wake," she offered.

"I will," he said. "But don't wait for me, because I might sleep off and won't like to be disturbed. I really appreciate your kind gesture, and thanks for your concern. Good night, Mrs. Montez."

"Good night," she replied. "And please, relax well. We will come and help with the cleaning tomorrow, so don't get yourself stressed. Now boys, say goodnight to Slim and thank him."

"Goodnight, Slim, and thank you," the boys echoed as they walked down the stairs with their mother. Slim walked them downstairs and shut the door behind them.

Chapter Three

Mrs. Montez

Mrs. Montez awoke very early the next morning. She had finished preparing breakfast for her boys, but she couldn't get off her mind the enigma she had experienced the previous day at Slim's place.

She had asked her boys if they had seen Slim make the bed when they had come in, and their replies confused her even more.

"He didn't make the bed," Jerald said. "It was still messy even before we left, wasn't it, Alex?"

"Yep, it was," Alex replied, still playing with his new PlayStation 3. He hadn't let go of it since he came home the previous night.

Mrs. Montez found it difficult to accept, and she found it even more difficult to believe it was all in her head. She decided to go check on him as she had promised. She arrived at his gate and what she saw astonished her even more. How could he have done it? It would take two professional gardeners a whole day to make his flowerbed look this good, but he had single-handedly done it overnight.

She decided to go around the house to see if he was still working on his garden because the house was quiet. She got to the backyard, and it was the same as the front; all the potatoes looked well weeded.

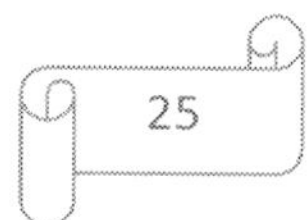

What is happening here? She kept asking herself. First, it was the bed in his room, and now the whole house looked cleaned up just overnight.

She would have quietly left, but on an impulse, she decided to check and see if he was really by himself or maybe someone was around and giving him a hand.

She stopped at his front door and listened to hear if there was any sound from inside, but the whole house was quiet. She reached out her hand to the bell and was about to ring it when the door opened. She almost fainted with fright, her face filled with fear.

"Oh my God, Slim! You almost scared me," she yelled, heaving a sigh of relief.

"Really?" he asked calmly. "Well, I'm sorry if I did. Besides, I didn't know you were at the door. I only thought I should come to take a look outside before I go take my breakfast, but thank goodness you're here. Come inside, Mrs. Montez, breakfast is ready."

She followed him, and she stood paralyzed at what she saw. The house was as clean and new as it looked when he first moved in some years back. She couldn't have forgotten when the young man first moved in after his family left the country. He had bought the house and had been staying here since then. Except at the time, he was not as creepy or weird as he seemed now, she thought to herself.

"How are the boys doing this morning?" he asked.

"Oh, you mean my kids! They're fine, I guess," she replied, her voice sounding a little choked. His question caught her, oblivious in her thought.

"Well, that is nice to hear," he replied as he walked to the dining table and poured himself some tea.

Mrs. Montez followed him to the table, and she was even more surprised to see that he had made a plate of hot pasta, chicken, and some sweet-scented fresh meat. This was too much of an enigma to her. She had just gone around the house a few minutes back, and everything was quiet. She could have perceived the aroma.

"So you made all this... and this morning?" she managed to ask, wondering to herself what mystery was happening here.

"Yes, of course. I took my time to prepare it," he said while still sipping his tea quietly.

"That was credible of you," she complimented. "And the cleaning also? I guess you did that as well."

"Oh, of course, I did that too. I couldn't get a good sleep, so I took the liberty to do the cleaning throughout the night," he replied casually.

"Hmm!" she mumbled with a sigh and chuckled. "And you did it all by yourself?" she asked again while looking at him amazedly. He nodded at her in affirmation. "Well, I see you have really become a machine," she complimented.

"Thanks for the compliment, Mrs. Montez. I must say I'm flattered," he said, stopping abruptly to observe her for a while. Then he pointed to the food. "You haven't touched your food," he said, pointing to the varieties on the table.

She regarded the food for a while. Though it looked well-cooked and delicious, she had always known he was a good cook. She wondered where he had gotten all those fresh delicacies that morning. As far as she was concerned, the grocery store had not yet opened. Besides that, even if he had gotten them from the store, he wouldn't have finished making them by now. Also, come to think of it, she never perceived any cooking or aroma some minutes ago, and even the whole house was as silent as a cemetery a few minutes ago. Just now, everything seemed to spring back to life. Something isn't right here, she perceived. She felt a little scared inside too. She dragged her gaze to meet Slim's, who was still sipping his coffee and quietly observing her as well.

She forced a smile at him, and he smiled back, pointing at the food again. "Oh! I'm okay," she said curtly. "I just finished breakfast before I came here. I just thought I should come to help you with the cleaning as I had promised, but I can see you've got it all under control." She stood to her feet, making an attempt to leave. "I must take my leave now. I've got to check on my boys; you know how mischievous they can be when left alone."

"Well, thanks for checking on me, but I'm most disappointed you never touched my food," he said with a soft grimace.

"Perhaps some other time," she retorted quickly and hurried with a quick stride toward the exit door before he drove her crazy. She got to the door, opened it, and suddenly yelled out an alarming scream that startled Slim as well.

He left his table and walked to her, wondering what could have startled her to scream. When he reached her, he burst out laughing. He saw Israel standing at the doorpost. She had opened the door and found him leaning on the post, which scared her as she wasn't expecting anyone there.

"Good morning, Mrs. Montez," Israel said. "What are you scared of? You look as if you've seen a ghost. Well, hope Anna and Clara are good?" he asked nonchalantly, not paying much attention to the frightened expression on her face.

"You guys aren't going to kill me," she managed to mutter under her breath, ignoring his question. She walked past him and stopped when she climbed down the stairs outside. "Thanks, Slim, for the gifts. My boys are really grateful," she said.

"You are most welcome, Mrs. Montez. Give them my regards," he replied.

Israel walked past him. "What did you do to her?" he asked casually. "I have never seen her this way before now. She looks real pale as if something in here frightened her."

Slim shrugged carelessly in response. "How can I know?" he replied while walking back to his breakfast.

"Well, I can see she has really helped you with the house cleaning, though I would have done it if you had informed me of your coming back earlier," Israel said. "However, it wouldn't have looked as tidy as this. It's really a woman's touch," he complimented with a cynical grin.

"Enough of your woman talk again!" Slim retorted jokingly. "I thought you would have grown out of it by now. Besides, she is old enough to be your mother." They both laughed at his joke and walked back to the dining table.

"Wow!" Israel exclaimed. "What a pleasant table! Thank goodness I came in time." Making himself comfortable, he scooped some pasta, added some meat to it, and carefully selected the best chicken. "This is delicious," he complimented.

Slim sat opposite him, sipping his tea quietly. "You never stop your gluttonous habits," he noted while watching him eat greedily.

"Say what you like, but I'm going to eat to my satisfaction," Israel replied while still eating the pasta and meat. "How is Mexico?" he asked.

"Same as it used to be, same old," Slim replied.

"I'm sure you really enjoyed Brazil, especially the carnival," Israel said while still helping himself to a piece of chicken.

Slim studied him quietly. "Yes, I did," he finally replied after a brief hesitation. "Rio was the best of carnivals. I really wish you had come. You would have seen the girls; they're really beautiful in diverse attires. The town was so colorful, full of people from all races. I can swear it was the best part of my life," he said, grimacing again.

"Stop talking nonsense," Israel cautioned him. "You sound as if your life has ended already. Besides, we can still go there this year, right?" he asked, now cleaning his hands and mouth with some tissue paper.

Slim laughed at that. "Maybe we might, and maybe not. But I'm not sure if we will be going together. You know we don't have all the time in this life," he added calmly.

"Quite thoughtful of you, but we are still young and full of life, so stop talking as if we are some old folks who will die any moment. Besides, I don't know when you suddenly became a philosopher," Israel reacted.

They both laughed at his joke. "So any plan for today?" Israel asked while standing and walking to the living room area. Slim followed him there.

"Yup, a lot of plans," Slim said. "Troy has been asking when you're going to return. He believes you always have these big ideas, coupled with the ones you must have gathered from Brazil. So I suggest we go see the guys first, and later we go see the girls, especially your girl Amanda. Man, she is damn hot now," he exclaimed with a whistle.

He paused and observed Slim for a brief moment. "Amanda? Why Amanda?" Slim asked, knowing fully well that Amanda was a phony and valued money mostly in relationships. He never really liked her. For all he knew, Amanda was only after his pocket. "So what happened to Samantha? Is she still in town? Because it's been a while since I last heard from her," he said.

Israel was quiet for a moment. "And what about that girl you told me about when you were in Brazil?" he asked, attempting to change the subject. "I thought you guys were deeply into something. I noticed she was always with you whenever we talked on the phone," he pointed out.

"Yup, we are in a serious relationship," Slim replied bluntly while pausing to study Israel again.

"Wow! That's nice," Israel retorted sharply.

"So back to my question," Slim said. "How is Samantha doing?" he asked again.

"Samantha! Samantha!! Well, she is fine, I guess," Israel replied, grimacing briefly. "Though she said you don't call her anymore, is that right?"

Slim shrugged and then asked, "Is that what she says? Well, we are both equally guilty of that. I hope she is good," he added bluntly.

"Yes, she is really doing well. Though she got engaged lately, I didn't want to tell you at first. I thought you should hear it from her first, now that you are here. However, you are my best friend, so it's good you heard it from me first. I guess she hasn't told you yet?"

"No, she never did. But that was brave of you to tell me. Though I suspected it when she stopped contacting me. That's why I decided to move on with Estella. But it's okay, no hard feelings. Besides, life goes on, and I am happy for her," Slim said with a grin.

They both sat quietly for a few minutes.

"Let's go out and catch some fun," Israel suggested, breaking the icy mood. "Or are we just going to stay in this hole all day long?" he asked.

"That's a good idea. Let me go upstairs; I need to freshen up and change into something new," Slim said. "I won't be long," he added.

"Take all the time you need," Israel replied. "I am quite sure you need much time to get that shabby look off you," he retorted back.

He stretched on one of the sofas, picked up the remote, and tuned to a music channel. A documentary would do better, he thought.

"Let's get going," Slim said emphatically. Israel almost jumped off the seat. He had never heard Slim walk down the stairs, and it hadn't even been three minutes since he left. How he took his bath and dressed so nicely in those few minutes really amazed him.

"You almost scared the hell out of me," he confessed. "And how did you change so soon?" he asked while staring at him in amazement. "Come on, I didn't get it. It hasn't even been a minute. I haven't even changed the channel, and you're done so soon."

"Let's go now," Slim said emphatically. "Besides, it's been about five minutes," he added.

Israel regarded him for a brief moment. They had been friends since childhood, and he didn't see anything wrong with him.

"Okay, let's go catch some fun," he said while picking up his car keys and walking with Slim to the door. They walked to where he had earlier parked his car outside the compound.

"You look great, Slim!" he complimented as he slid into the driver's seat of his Ferrari, with Slim sitting beside him in the passenger seat. He ignited the car and zoomed off.

Chapter Four

TROY

Troy sat on the staircase outside Israel's place, watching as Israel cleaned his Ferrari. It had been a week since Slim came back. A lot had happened during that time; they had gone to several clubs, beaches, and parties in the town.

Today, Troy had come to see Israel, though it was still early. He had been a little quiet and thoughtful since he arrived.

"Have you seen Slim since yesterday?" he asked.

"Nope, but we spoke this morning. He said he had some business deals to settle in town, but he will come around during the day," Israel replied casually while still polishing his car rims. "Anything the problem?" he asked, now done with the cleaning and walking to join Troy where he sat. "Why are you so full of thought, dude?" he asked.

Troy shrugged and heaved a brief sigh. "Nothing really," he replied, pausing for a split second, meditating on where to start. "You know you are closer to Slim than I am," he started to say. "Even though Slim and I are from the same country, and he is much like a brother to me," he added, then halted.

Israel studied him for a moment with a grin. "I hope you don't mean to tell me that you are jealous of our friendship?" he asked, pausing briefly. "But come to think of it, why would you say that?"

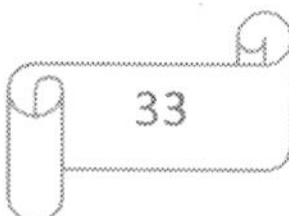

"As I have earlier said, it is nothing of much importance. Though I am only curious about something, but never mind, maybe it's just my perception."

"And what is this perception about?" Israel asked curiously, gazing intently at Troy, who seemed a little undecided yet.

Troy scratched his hair for a while, then turned to Israel. "You know I respect Slim, and I really adore his sense of reasoning, especially when it comes to variation and logical reasoning." He stopped again while observing Israel, who seemed a bit confused.

"I suggest you hit the bull by the eye, because I am yet to fathom what you are trying to say here. But as far as I am concerned, he hasn't changed in that respect either," Israel corrected.

"I quite agree with you," Troy replied thoughtfully. "Except for the fetish and diabolic ideas he now professes," he pointed out. "And as the saying goes, a leopard doesn't change its spots overnight."

Israel sat up, studying Troy for a brief moment. "You know what I think? You sound even more mystical in your words than the fetish you spoke about. Besides, what is it that you noticed that makes you think he has changed?"

"He talks in riddles lately, especially about African voodoo beliefs, although he has never been to Africa. Which makes me a little scared and uncomfortable with him," Troy said.

Israel laughed historically at him for a moment. "Is that all? You forgot he just got back from Brazil. Besides, if I know Slim as much as I think I do, I would say he is a xenophile. He easily adopts cultures. Aside from that, Brazilian culture is almost similar to that of the Africans."

"Oh, I almost forgot that part. I should have thought of that," Troy said. "But you know something? Last time we saw a cat, I tried chasing it, especially since it appeared from nowhere, and you couldn't have imagined how scared of those creatures I can be.

However, Slim asked me to let it be. He said that cats are mystic animals and they have the ability to heal," he explained and paused briefly with a quick grin. "I would have taken that as just a mere myth if not for what happened last night," he added.

At this point, Israel was up, listening and watching him more attentively. "So what happened last night?" he asked anxiously.

"You know Jessica, my little sister, was down with a fever for the last two days. However, it was so severe last night that I was wondering if she was ever going to make it till dawn."

"Really? But you should have called me. I would have come to help take her to the hospital. I thought it was just a mere cold that she had," Israel said, feeling a little guilty within himself, especially as he had not asked about her health earlier. "So how is she doing now?" he asked casually.

"She is good now," Troy said. "Do you think I would have come out here if she wasn't okay yet? Well, it all happened so quickly that her sudden recovery was weird to me," he added.

"Why was her recovery so weird to you?" Israel asked curiously, sitting perplexed. He really didn't understand why the conversation had to start with Slim as the subject.

"Well, that's where I'm heading," Troy replied casually. "She was sweating profusely and having pain all over. I called the hospital, and they told me all the doctors were off duty at the time. To further complicate things, they said no ambulance was available at the moment either. As that was the case, I had no choice but to treat her on my own. So I started using a towel and water to clean off the sweat from her face, an old trick I learned from Mama," he said.

He paused again while watching Israel, who seemed much more interested in where he was heading. "Well, she finally slept, and I dozed off on the chair as well," he said.

Israel grimaced at him for a while, already getting impatient with the long story. "So what happened? Because I'm sure you aren't going to tell me Slim came in and healed her?"

Troy shook his head wearily. "No, he never did. However, I was awoken when she screamed, 'Cat!' And you know I don't like cats. I almost ran out of the room. A black cat was lying by her side. Jessica, who is a lover of animals, kept stroking the mystery creature. She later asked me to come and take it out. I was so scared to the core. And guess who called at that moment?"

Israel shrugged carelessly. "You know I'm not a good guesser, and I'm sure you know that already. And you know what? You're scaring me already as well. Where did the cat come from? And how did it end up on Jessica's bed?"

Troy chuckled briefly. "Well, that was exactly what I was asking myself at that moment. However, Slim called at that moment. He said he just wanted to know how Jessica was doing."

"Wow! That's nice of him. So I guess you told him the story, and he came over to help, right?"

Troy shrugged again. "No, he didn't come over. He only sounded even weirder. I told him what had happened, and he asked me if the animal ran when she woke up. I told him no, that it just lay there beside her. And he said that was a good sign, that she was going to be okay by dawn."

Israel heaved a sigh of relief. "He said so, and she was okay by dawn, right? Umm... hmm... So Slim is now becoming a seer," he mumbled jokingly. "Well, it all sounds good to me. You should be thanking him and stop making something out of nothing. It's just logical reasoning. I could have done the same," he added.

Troy shrugged at him and continued. "Well, the cat was gone by dawn, and by morning, Jessica was really okay. You wouldn't have believed she was ever sick the previous night."

"Well, I'm happy for Jessica. At least she is okay now. But seriously, I don't see anything wrong with Slim's assumption. He was just a caring friend," Israel said, pausing briefly. "Can we just forget about all this crazy talk and change the subject if you don't mind? Or maybe we just go grab some drinks to celebrate Jessica's recovery. Is that okay?" he asked.

"Sounds good to me as well," Troy agreed. "So let's go now."

He stood to his feet and joined Israel. They both walked to the Ferrari and rode to the city municipal.

Chapter Five

A DRIVE TO THE AGENCY

Israel arrived at Slim's place. He parked his car in the parking space while still seated inside. He honked for Slim to come out, and a minute later, Mayan came out accompanied by Slim.

"Hey Israel," she said. "What brings you out here this early?" she asked, smiling at him.

"Hello, beauty!" he complemented, though he noticed that she looked a little pale. "When did you arrive here?" he asked curiously, surprised to see her around.

She chuckled at him. "Last night, though I just came here this morning to get some of my stuff. I will be leaving by noon," she said.

"Well, that is good," he said. "Slim never told me you would be coming. I guess you must have been doing all the house chores since morning," he said to her. Turning to Slim, he added, "Well, come on Slim, let's go now. We are getting late already. I can see you've got a hand around."

Slim walked to Mayan and gave her a peck on the cheek, then walked down to Israel who was still sitting in the car. He jumped into the car, as it was in a convertible mode, thereby not using the door. He slid into the passenger seat beside Israel, making himself

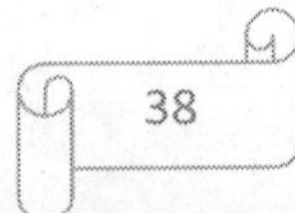

comfortable. He turned to Israel, who was staring furiously at him for not using the door. "Let's go," he said.

"Next time, use the door!" Israel squabbled at Slim as he fastened his seat belt. He reversed the car out of the parking space, then turned to Mayan. "Okay, Mayan," he said. "I will come back to check on you later. Slim and I have to go to the state agency now. I guess he already told you."

Mayan stood there speechless, watching him as he drove out of the gate and onto the freeway. Her expression astonished him. He observed that she started acting weird after he asked Slim to hurry up.

"Did I say something I'm not supposed to, Slim? Or maybe I came at the wrong time?" he asked. "I don't understand why she was gazing at me in bewilderment. One minute she was smiling, and the next, an attitude. Come on, Slim! I didn't get it," he complained.

Slim smiled at him mildly. "Women! They can be that temperamental. They are really hard to understand sometimes. But never mind her attitude. Perhaps you just reminded her of something that got her emotional. Let's put this aside and stop making something out of nothing," he said.

Israel shrugged curtly. "Well, I agree with you," he said. "So how long will you be staying at the agency?" he asked, trying to change the subject, which seemed absurd to him.

Slim giggled at him. "An hour, maybe more," he replied. "However, it depends on how fast I'm attended to."

"An hour!" Israel exclaimed. "That's quite some time. So I have to stay outside waiting for you all that time? Oh no! I wish you had come with your car instead of putting me through all this stress," he said.

Slim regarded him for a while with a quick grimace. "Next time, I will do just that," he replied firmly, his voice a little shrill. "I'm sure that way I won't have to bother you for this again," he added.

"Come on, Slim! Don't give me that attitude now! You know I'm only kidding. I don't mean anything I just said. You are my best friend, and I owe you a lot. Besides, I'd gladly wait a year out here for you," he said jokingly.

They both laughed in reaction to his joke for a moment. "Well, there is a coffee shop outside the agency building. You can hang out there while I'm inside. I'm sure you will catch some fun in there, and probably you wouldn't even remember you are waiting for me," Slim said.

"That will do," Israel replied as they arrived at the big agency building. Slim opened the door and walked to the entrance, and Israel drove to the sideway and parked there. He walked back to the café and waited.

It had been an hour and thirty minutes now, so he strolled back to where he had earlier parked his car. However, there was no sign of Slim anywhere near, except for the security guard he had seen there when they had come in earlier. He decided to wait inside the car.

"Are you waiting for someone?" a voice asked him out of the blue. He raised his gaze to meet the young security guard he had seen earlier, standing by his car.

"Oh yes, I am!" he retorted sharply. "I am waiting for the guy I came here with two hours earlier. You remember him, right? Well, he went in there to do some documentation. I don't know why he has taken so long," he said. Just then, he saw Slim coming down the stairway from the agency building.

"Oh! There he comes," he said, pushing open the passenger door to let Slim in as he got closer. Slim slid into the car and shut the door after him.

"Thanks," Slim said to the guard. "We will be leaving now." He ignited the car and moved to the main road, leaving the guard staring astonished after him.

"What was that about again?" Israel asked Slim. "Did you see how that guy was staring at me? Or am I wearing some creepy looks that you aren't telling me about?" he asked again, checking himself in the side mirror.

Slim yelled out a cynical laugh. "Nothing is wrong with you, buddy. I believe you are just imagining things," he said.

"Do you think so?" Israel asked, still examining himself in the mirror. "He was the second person giving me that weird look today," he added.

"Well, I still believe it's all in your head," Slim repeated. "Besides, how would you know if he wasn't staring at me?" he asked, pausing for a moment and watching Israel as he drove in silence. "By the way, I will be traveling tomorrow," he added.

"Really! You do a lot of traveling lately. I hope you won't be gone long this time around?" Israel asked.

"I can't really tell," Slim replied. "Can't tell how long," he repeated as they drove back toward his place.

Chapter Six

Amanda

Amanda Romero was doing some shopping at a mall. She had run out of cash and needed some good cash to meet her needs. She got some cosmetics on credit and promised to come back to settle the debt later on. Amanda was a materialistic girl, always jumping on rich boys for money. She was one of those girls known as a social climber.

She picked up her stuff and walked to the exit door of the big mall. And as she waits for a taxi, she saw him. "Wow! Slim," she thought to herself. "So he is back in town, and he didn't even bother to call or contact me?" she marveled. He seems absent minded, driving in his favorite car, a Jaguar.

She had wanted to call him, but he drove so fast and seemed absent-minded.

"Hmm! Slim, so you're back in town? Well, I will get to you today," she muttered to herself. She stopped a cab and hurried home to drop her provisions.

Some minutes later, she was at Slim's mansion. She let herself in as the gate was left wide open, and she was sure he was inside. The flowers were as beautiful and clean as they used to be, and they seemed to shimmer with an ethereal glow. She liked him but loved his cheerful life better, especially the way he spoiled her with money.

As she walked down the lane to his front door, she noticed the house looked quiet as if no one was inside. However, she was certain he was heading home when she had seen him, for he couldn't have gone elsewhere. He was a quiet guy who loved the serenity of his house. She rang the glockenspiel and waited, but there was still no sign of anyone coming. Why was the gate open? She was quite sure he was around, or maybe he was asleep. She decided to walk to the backyard to see if she could see anything from there.

As she moved away from the door, she heard voices coming from the backyard, and suddenly a lot of activity. She could clearly hear Slim's voice giving out orders, as if he was summoning enchanted helpers to assist him. It seemed as if some boys were doing some work for him. She wondered how come she never heard all those noises some minutes ago. Perhaps her obsession to get into the house had prevented her from hearing the noise.

She walked in that direction and then saw him. He looked handsome as usual, watching a group of boys who seemed to glide effortlessly, as if guided by an unseen force, doing his garden weeding.

"Okay boys, let me go get you something to drink inside. I'm sure you boys must be exhausted by now," he said.

He turned and saw Amanda coming his way. "Wow, Amanda!" he exclaimed. "What a pleasant surprise."

She smiled at him and walked toward him. "I was just passing by and saw your gate open, so I decided to see who was inside since you never told me you'd be coming back," she said, walking to him and giving him a firm hug.

"I'm sorry about that," he apologized while letting himself free from her grip. He held her closer and planted a passionate kiss on her cheek. "I never knew I would be around myself," he said. "It just caught me by surprise, and I had no choice but to come here. However, it's nice seeing you around again. Now let's go inside," he said, holding her by the wrist and walking her to the front door of his house.

Meanwhile, inside the house, he asked, "What can I offer you, beauty?" teasing her. "You know I wouldn't mind going to the moon for you. So just name it! Your wish is my command."

She smiled at him sheepishly. That's the one thing she really loved about him; his kind gesture. He really knew how to treat a lady. "Just get me something chilled," she said.

He reached into the refrigerator and brought out two chilled cans of beer. "Feel at home," he said. "Let me get the boys something to drink," he added.

He walked to the refrigerator again and took out several cans of chilled soft drinks in a basket he had brought from the kitchen. "Give me just a few moments, please; I will be with you in a moment," he said. Leaning closer, he planted a soft kiss on her cheek again and walked to the door, leaving her behind.

Some minutes later, he wasn't back, so she made an effort to go check on him. Just then, she heard some cooking from his kitchen. 'Had he gone through the back door to surprise her?' she thought to herself. She went towards the kitchen to check on what he was doing but was surprised to see a middle-aged woman cooking. The woman had already finished making some sweet-smelling dishes.

"Oh, I'm sorry for barging in on you like this. It's just that Slim never told me anyone was around," she apologized.

"Never mind," the strange woman replied. "He is busy lately. He asked me to make the boys some food. However, he asked that I serve you first. So just go have your seat, and I'll bring yours over right away."

She walked back to her seat and sat down quietly, wondering why Slim never told her about this arrangement and his strange guest. She believed the woman could either be his aunt or some house help. This lady wasn't his kind of woman; besides, she was close to being his mother, she thought, consoling herself.

Some minutes later, she had finished eating, and still no sign of Slim. She strolled outside to the garden. However, the boys were still working at it, but there was no sign of him anywhere. She walked to one of the boys, who was still busy with the cabbage.

"Hey!" she said. "Please, where did Slim go?" she asked curiously. This was not his habit; she was surprised at how he had left her for so long and especially now, at his sudden disappearance.

She was angry with the boy as he was still checking on the cabbage and deliberately ignoring her. "What a brat?" she muttered; she hated kids, they annoyed her with their attitudes.

"I am talking to you, brat," she yelled at him and simultaneously grabbed the boy's face to meet hers.

But she immediately drew back at what she saw. It horrified her so much that she nearly choked. As she drew back from him, a potato shrub trapped her foot, making her lose her balance. She stood up and ran blindly back to the house, screaming with fright.

"Slim! Slim!!" she yelled out in fright as she ran toward the entrance of the house. "Those boys are faceless," she said while screaming in fear as she opened the door and entered the house.

She got into the living room in no time, and the atmosphere was calm. This scared her even more. The house was quiet and cold, with no aroma of the food that had earlier overwhelmed the room. The table looked as if it had not been used for quite a long time.

"Slim!" she managed to mutter under her breath, with a frightened expression written all over her face.

And then she saw him coming down the staircase. She ran to him and hugged him tightly.

"What is happening here?" she screamed while yelling at him. "Your boys and the cook? They're all strange! Please get me out of here," she pleaded.

"Calm down," he said. "What boys are you talking about, and what cook? I don't have a cook. Besides, I just came in now, and I didn't even know you were around," he retorted sharply at her.

She watched him with doubt, with fright written all over her face. "Stop the joke! Don't play pranks on me," she yelled while screaming at him. She turned and ran to the kitchen. She got there and stood amazed at what she saw. The kitchen looked nasty and messy, as if it had not been used in a century.

"I told you I don't have a cook," he said coldly from behind.

She almost screamed in fear at the sound of his voice; she felt haunted. She had run here, leaving him in the living room, wanting to prove to him that he had a cook. However, she never heard or saw him coming after her. How was he suddenly behind her? It scared her even more.

"I told you, I never had a cook," he said again calmly while attempting to touch her face.

"Get away from me!" she screamed at him. At the same time, she moved away, running toward the exit door of the house, and attempting to open the door, which handle seemed to have stuck now. She tried forcing the handle open with no success as he came closer. She was so scared that she started screaming loudly for help. Then, the door opened, and everything went calm again as before.

Meanwhile, outside the house, she stood speechless. She was welcomed only by the sight of Slim driving in from the entrance toward the house. He was in his Jaguar, as she had earlier seen him at the mall. Then who was it that she was with the entire time inside?

She watched him park the car in his parking space, and he waved and smiled admiringly at her from inside the car. At that point, her feet felt weak and hardly supported her weight. She slumped down and fainted.

Chapter Seven

Samantha

Samantha Rodriguez stood outside Slim's place at the west end; she observed the house for a while. It had been a while since she had been here, and she wondered if he was around. A friend had told her earlier that day that she had seen him, and she had decided to come pay him a visit. Although she knew he no longer considered her his girlfriend and she would be wedded soon, she hadn't informed him of that since he had stayed long in Brazil and had changed a lot. He had even stopped contacting her.

She wondered if he was holding a grudge against her for not waiting for him, knowing for certain that his best friend Israel must have informed him of the latest development. Although it wasn't her fault, she thought to herself, using that as an excuse to console herself. They had dated for two years, and in all that time, he had never proposed to marry her or tried to engage her. She believed he must have gotten fed up with the relationship and decided to move on, and she had done the same as well. As for her current fiancé, they had barely spent two months together, and he had already proposed to and engaged her, and now they would be wedded soon. Nevertheless, it was unlike Slim to hold a grudge or snub her. He was mature in handling issues, perhaps not relationship stuff. She had learned that he had been in town for quite a while now, and in all that time, he had not bothered contacting her. She had decided to see him in person and set things straight; at least they should be on good terms, even if they were no longer dating.

She had dressed up for work very early that evening, as she would be resuming her shift duty post as a nurse by 20:00. It was just 18:20 now, so she must have been done by 19:40, and it wouldn't take her twenty minutes to get to her workplace from here.

She observed the house closely again; however, it looked lifeless, even though the gate to the main building was half-open. It was already evening, and darkness was approaching faster. The lights downstairs all seemed to be out, except for the light on the lamp standing outside the building and the one by the drive lane leading from the gate to the main house.

The taxi driver honked at her, as she had stood there for about five minutes now, oblivious of the taxi she had taken down here.

"Oh! I'm sorry," she said, apologizing to the old gentleman who had been so kind and waited patiently for her all the while. "It's just that I don't think anyone is inside. The light in the building seems out. I don't think Slim likes sitting in the dark all alone," she explained her plight to the kind driver.

"Well, should I take you back?" he asked. "Or maybe you go in and check on him, and I will wait here," he suggested, trying to be of help to her while scanning the building to see if he could spot any sign of life.

"Thanks!" she replied. "I think I should just hurry in and do just that," she said, stopping abruptly as the driver gestured at her.

"I think someone is in there," he retorted. "There is a light on the top floor, and I think I saw a man's figure by the window just now."

She turned and regarded the house again, and this time she saw a light on the first floor, in a room she knew was Slim's. She noticed a figure walking past the window and recognized him at once. She smiled at the driver, paid her fare, and left the change for the kind old man. The driver was of good help to her, and the taxi drove away, leaving her behind.

She stood there undecided for a moment while staring at the house again. She was sure that the whole house looked dead a few minutes ago, except for the light outside. As far as she was concerned, Slim never put out the light in his room while he was in. She wondered what had changed now. She helped herself through the half-closed gate and walked down the lane to the main building.

Now at the doorpost, she stopped, feeling a little naïve and awkward about doing this. She checked her wristwatch; it was already 18:55. She wondered how time had run so fast today. She rang the doorbell and waited for him to come down. A few minutes later, there was no sound of any movement from inside. However, she was sure she had seen him upstairs by the window. She made an attempt to ring the bell again, and then she heard a voice.

"Hmm umm, I can't believe who I'm seeing at my doorpost," a voice said from behind her.

She turned quickly, almost freezing from the fright of seeing him behind her. She had seen him a while ago upstairs from outside the house. She had come here, and all the while, no movement inside. How did he suddenly get behind her? It was a mystery to her.

"Aw!" she said, yelling out a light scream of shock at him. "You startled me. And how did you get down here so quick? I just saw you upstairs."

He stopped and grinned at her for a moment. "Is that how you're supposed to say hi to me even after all this while?" he asked. She climbed down the stairs of his doorpost, walked to him, and gave him a hug.

"Oh, sorry! I lost my good manners. I missed you," she said.

"I missed you too," he replied calmly. "I can see you're in your uniform. Are you on a night shift, or are you just coming back from the hospital?" he asked, shaking his head at her. "That I doubt, because you smell fresh," he added.

She grimaced at him briefly and let out a smile. "You're never going to change," she said jokingly. "Well, I'm on my way to work, because I'm on a night shift this week. So I decided to check on you before I resumed my duty post since you have decided to cut me off permanently," she replied bluntly and paused briefly. "But seriously, how did you get down here? I never heard you coming. Besides, I saw you upstairs a while ago, by the window while I was coming in."

"I wasn't in," he replied firmly, cutting her mid-speech. "I was just coming in from a stroll. I was surprised to see a lady at my doorpost, so I crept behind to see who it was. And I was surprised to see that it was you," he said.

She stared inquisitively at him briefly. "I'm sure I saw you upstairs. Do you have anyone around?" she asked.

"No," he replied. "I haven't started sharing the house yet. However, I'm sure it's just your imagination. Besides, the keys are here with me," he said, simultaneously bringing out some keys and showing them to her.

She paused for a while and moved a few paces from the building. She gazed upward; the house looked quiet, except for the light. She knew what she had seen and could have sworn it was him. "Well, maybe it was my imagination," she admitted, seeing no point in arguing.

"Would you like to go in and chill out?" he asked. She smiled at him and quickly checked her wristwatch, which read 19:35.

"Oh my God!" she exclaimed. "I guess I should be on my way now. I wonder how time flew so quickly today."

He grinned at her. "Well, they do sometimes, and they fly so fast that they leave us no time to ourselves," he retorted philosophically.

She studied him for a while; "you are right," she agreed, "will you walk me to the road now," "at least, I have seen you." she said.

They walk toward the gate in a slow and quiet stride; "I just came to let you know in person," "that I will soon be getting wedded." She said, breaking the ice.

"Congratulations!!" He replied.
She stops and observed him for a moment;
"Are you mad at me?" She asked calmly.

"And why should I be mad at you?" he asked with a sneering expression on his face. "Besides, it's a good decision you made."

"But you don't seem happy with it," she retorted sharply. He shrugged and went quiet again.

"And all this was your fault, you know? You stopped calling me. You gave me the impression," she said.

"For God's sake, Sam! It's just been six months!" he retorted back. "Besides, when was the last time you called or even checked on me?" he asked bluntly.

By now, the evening was already dark, and the lamppost light seemed too blurry for her to make out his face as they walked toward the gate. Something seemed indistinct here; his face seemed to be covered by some gloomy shadow, and she tried to figure it out. This scared her a little, especially with his strange attitude.

"That would be around the last four months," she replied, still trying to figure out the trace of his face.

"Well, that would be enough time for a corpse to have decomposed," he said.

At that point, sudden lightning began to strike, illuminating his face. She jerked back at what she saw; it was the worst grotesque sight she had ever seen in her life, even as a nurse. His face was a half-human, rotten skull entwined with worms eating it, and he looked half putrefying. She screamed and withdrew quickly from his side.

"Who are you?" she asked while drawing back from him. However, he kept walking toward her. "Stay away from me!" she screamed in shock and ran toward the gate, which looked closed now. She struggled with the iron gate to no avail.

"It's still me, sweetheart," she heard his voice say from behind her. She could perceive an awful smell all around her as he spoke.

"Don't touch me!" she screamed in fear as she continued struggling with the gate. She heard him laughing scornfully, which frightened her so much that she fell down and fainted.

**   ***   **

"Wake up!" she heard a soft feminine voice say to her while tapping her gently on her shoulder.

"Don't touch me, please," she protested while screaming faintly.

"Wake up, Samantha! Are you having a nightmare in the office?"

She opened her eyes wearily and saw Candice staring at her. "What is it with you, girlfriend?" Candice asked. "I have been watching over you here for over fifteen minutes now. I had to wake you up when I couldn't take it anymore."

Samantha looked around the environment and realized she was at the hospital, in the nurse's dressing room. She was surprised to see that she had slept on one of the tables facing a mirror, with her head on her arms. "How did I get here?" she asked.

"Excuse me?" Candice said. "Are you okay, girlfriend?" she asked while staring inquisitively at her.

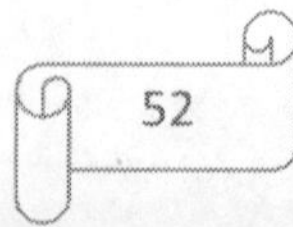

"How did I get here?" Samantha asked again.

"Well, girlfriend, I don't know what is up with you today. Perhaps too much stress from school, home, and then work, coupled with the marriage preparations. I can't tell. But if you must know, I came in here and found you sleeping all by yourself. Besides, Camilla told me you came in earlier today. I checked and saw you signed in around 18:20, and I began to wonder if your home is suddenly beginning to bite you," Candice added.

Samantha checked her wristwatch, and it was just 18:55, which was the same time she had arrived at Slim's doorpost. "This can't be true," she said soberly. "What day is today?" she asked again.

Candice stared at her suspiciously. "Are you running some kind of fever, girlfriend?" she asked, simultaneously using her hand to feel Samantha's body temperature. She observed her friend again and shook her head.

"Well, today is Wednesday, the 24th of August. But why are you acting so weird, girlfriend?" she managed to ask. "Are you going nuts from your dream or something? Because you're acting like someone on coke," she said, pausing to observe her for a moment again. "Okay now, tell me what this dream is all about."

Samantha shrugged wearily. "It wasn't a dream," she said carelessly. "Though I don't know what happened or how I got here, but it was all him."

Candice moved closer to her curiously. "Him? Who do you mean by him?" she asked.

"Slim!" Samantha retorted.

"Oh! Wow... you mean to say that your handsome Mexican ex-boyfriend? Oh my gosh! What I wouldn't give just to have him chase me around, even if it was only in a dream," Candice exclaimed while crossing her arms over her chest and caressing herself in a girlish gesture.

"Well, not in that form, Candice!" Samantha retorted with a grimace, heaving a sigh. "He looked weird and grotesque."

"That must be serious," Candice said as she walked closer to Samantha, who narrated the event to her while she sat quietly, listening the whole time.

"Well, it was such a horrible dream," Candice finally said. "But could that mean that he is dead?"

"It's not a dream," Samantha retorted firmly. "Besides, it's been a while since I last contacted him. I lost his contact, so I can't tell where he is now."

 "Well, it is all a dream, girlfriend. Now cut the drama. Though it may sound weird, it is all just a dream," Candice replied firmly. "Aside from that, let's assume it was real. Could he have turned back the hand of time? Or carried you in here and signed in your signature for you?" she asked. "Now let's check your time," she said. Samantha checked her wristwatch, and it read 19:35, the same time she had asked Slim to see her off.

"Well, I don't understand the enigma behind this, but it was so real. I could swear it was real. I could still perceive that awful smell coming from him, even now," Samantha said.

"Well, some dreams are like that, girlfriend. They feel so real, but in the end, they are just dreams. So I suggest you get over it before someone thinks you're going nuts," Candice said, hesitating for a moment. "Now let's go get something to eat at the cafeteria. It's almost time to resume our duty shift," she pointed out.

"Okay," Samantha agreed. As they made to leave, she noticed a bruise on her shoulder. She remembered she had sustained the injury when she had fallen at Slim's gate. Candice noticed the bruise too.

"Girl, that must hurt. How could you have slept with that? Now, hurry, let's go so I can dress it up for you," Candice said.

Samantha stood on her feet and grabbed her handbag from the table where she had rested. In doing so, something fell from beneath the bag, and the two girls stared amazed at the object for a while. It was a necklace that Slim had given her when they had first started dating, with a picture of him and her engraved on it. She had lost it a few months ago.

"I thought you said you'd lost that thing, girlfriend," Candice remarked.

"Yes, I did," Samantha replied sharply.

"So how did it get here, stuck under your handbag?" Candice asked.

Samantha shrugged while still staring at the necklace in surprise. "If I told you I knew how it got here, I'd be lying," she retorted sharply.

"So are we going to get it now, or are you just going to keep staring at it? I want it, girlfriend, that is if you don't," Candice said.

"Let's leave it here," Samantha replied firmly.

"But I said I want it," Candice retorted in a stuttered tone.

"Candice, not now, please. I said let's leave it here."

"Okay, if you say so. As you wish, girlfriend. Now hurry, let's go fix up your bruises," Candice said.

"Sounds good," Samantha replied, and they both walked a couple of steps out of the dressing room. But Samantha stopped abruptly. "On second thought, I guess I should return it to him," she said.

She turned and walked back with a quick stride to the dressing room, with Candice a couple of steps behind her. They soon got back to the spot where she had left the object, and both girls stood there amazed. No one could have entered the room, as they had not even taken ten steps outside. However, now the necklace was gone and it was nowhere to be found.

"Where is it? I thought we left it here, girlfriend?" Candice asked in surprise.

Samantha nodded her head and shrugged coldly. "Let's go, or else we will be late for dinner."

Candice stood there amazed for a moment, wondering what mystery had just taken place.

She finally nodded her head in agreement with Samantha's suggestion. For the first time since the conversation, she started to reconsider her friend's dream; perhaps it wasn't a dream after all, she thought to herself.

"Let's go, girlfriend," she finally said.

Chapter Eight

Israel and Mayan

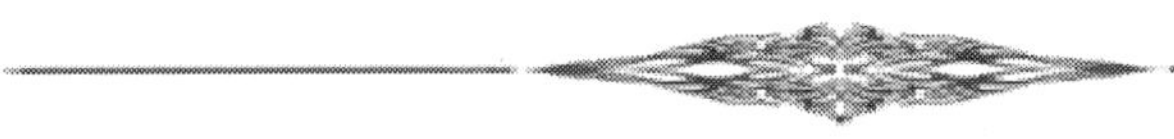

Israel drove past Slim's place and was surprised to see a 'TO-LET' sign at the front of the house. What is this about, he pondered within himself. He parked his car and walked to inspect the house. However, Mrs. Montez and her children had gone on vacation. As he stood there, he saw Mayan coming out of the house. She had some stuff with her and was about to bolt the door.

"Hi Mayan," he said to her as she came out of the house. "What's up with you? What is it with the sign outside? Isn't Slim coming back again?" he asked while gazing inquisitively at her. "He told me he is not going to be long. I'm surprised to see you putting this sign outside his place. Please, what is all this about?" he inquired.

She stood there amazed, regarding him for a brief moment. Her reaction pissed him off, and he began to feel insulted and uncomfortable with her attitude toward him lately.

She made an attempt to move away from him, but on impulse, she stood still. Then, leaning on one of the supportive pillars, she stared at him with a frown.

"I thought, even if you wouldn't have come to pay us a condolence, at least you should have enough decency to respect his memory," she said with a dark grimace.

Her last words left him breathless. They struck him like an arrow to the heart, and he felt weak and paralyzed for a moment.

"I don't understand what you mean here, Mayan. I mean the pay your condolence or respect his memory stuff you just said now. For God's sake! He just traveled two days back, and now you're telling me he is a memory?" he stuttered.

She gave him a disdainful look. "Are you for real? And are we really talking about my brother Nickerson?" she asked with a contemptuous gaze.

Israel felt uncomfortable and began to sweat profusely. He looked confused and dismayed. "Yes, of course!" he retorted sharply. "He is the only person here; everyone in this neighborhood knows him as Slim, and I'm sure you are aware of that too."

She stood still for a moment, then brushed her hair backward while watching him with a bewildered gaze. "Nick died a month ago in a car accident. He was on his way to the airport to board a plane to the U.S. when it happened. So, I'm surprised you keep mentioning his name anytime you see me around here. It offends me much and makes me think you're playing with my intelligence."

"No! No!! No!!!" he interrupted, even before she concluded what she was saying. "I think it is you playing with my intelligence. I dropped Slim the other day at the airport. Aside from that, two days ago, I came here, and you guys came out of the house together. I took him to the agency. He even gave you a peck, and I told you I would be back soon to check on you. I'm sure you remember that, right?" he asked anxiously, looking confused and astonished at her.

She studied him for a brief moment. She thought to herself that she had to move away from this guy; he was not well, she perceived.

"Well, I don't know what you're talking about," she said calmly. And she narrated the entire incident to him and stopped, grimacing at him, her voice now sounding a little choked. "I suggest you get his image off your head," she advised firmly. "Nick is dead and buried long ago. But if you still doubt me, come home with me to Mexico. I will show you his grave. I've got to go now. You can shut the door when you're leaving," she added in an attempt to avoid the conversation, as it upset her. She walked to the road and took a taxi, leaving him behind.

Israel stood there, paralyzed. He didn't believe a word she just said. Perhaps she was going nuts, he thought to himself. Or perhaps Slim had now gone into some mischievous activities and was trying to cover his tracks, playing dead, even after all the people that had seen him here. He wished Mrs. Montez was around. "Oh!" he said, remembering something. He needed to prove her wrong. He rushed to his car and drove to the agency.

**   ***   **

Dr. Robert was in his living room, reading some papers when Mayan walked in. She had the stuff she had gone to get from her brother's place. Dr. Robert Malone was a distant relative of her dad, and they often visited him during their vacations, especially as he had no children of his own and regarded them as his.

"You can't believe that guy Israel," she said as she walked into the living room. "I guessed he must be going crazy or something like that. He kept saying he saw Nick, and he even says he saw us together, and Nick even gave me a peck in his presence. He was so obsessed with Nick that he believed he was still in town. I was so fed up with him that I had to put him in his place. At least he should respect his memory and let him be," she said emphatically while walking to a big couch and sitting down, facing the older man.

 Dr. Robert regarded her thoughtfully for a while. "So Israel also has a story as well, hmm? Well, there have been many ghost tales lately," he said.

She sat up and faced him, wondering what story he was referring to.

"A girl was rushed to the hospital yesterday. She was found lying unconscious at the west end of Santa Clara. I guess it's close to where Nick stays. She said it was a ghost. She also mentioned a lot of things I could not make any sense of, like something about faceless boys in the garden and a guy she called Slim turning multiple!" He halted and observed Mayan briefly. He noticed she was nonchalant about his story. "Well," he continued, "she's okay now, I guess," he concluded.

However, Mayan sat up abruptly and gazed at him. She had not been paying attention to what he was saying until he mentioned the name Slim.

"And what was the name of this girl?" she asked with genuine interest.

Dr. Robert stared at her for a moment. "Why are you suddenly interested in her name?" he asked. "Well, though I didn't get her last name, she goes by the name Amanda. Do you happen to know her?" he asked.

"That bitch!" she retorted angrily. "She'd messed him up while he was alive, and yet she still can't help making a story of him even now that he has passed on," she said.

"You just insulted her," the older man noted. "Do you happen to know her?" he asked again while still staring at her. "And please don't tell me that Nick was the same person as Slim, because I don't seem to understand what is pissing you off here."

Mayan sat disturbed for a moment and then turned to the older man. "Nick was nicknamed Slim in the west end. Everyone there never knew him as Nick, but they only knew him as Slim there. And Amanda happens to be a girl he used to date back then. Officially, they weren't dating and never broke up; they were just friends with benefits. However, he got fed up with her because she kept using

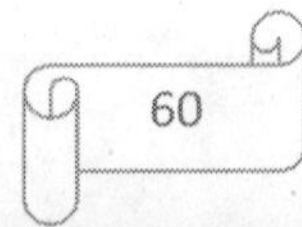

him as an extra pocket. I'm quite sure she is making up those stories."

Mrs. Malone came in and joined them. She had been in the kitchen preparing dinner and had been half-listening to their conversation. She came in and sat close to Mayan. "Don't you think it is strange, my dear?" she asked Mayan while holding her hands. "Everyone who says they saw him never called him by his real name," she noted.

Mayan sat still for a moment, feeling uncomfortable with the subject. "Now don't tell me you believe any of that stuff too?" she asked with a grimace while standing to her feet. "I don't know who or what they believe they have seen, but whatever it was, I don't give a damn about it and care less to know. However, I'm quite sure it isn't my brother because I watched him die, and he was buried right before my very eyes," she said and hesitated for a moment. "I've got to shower; I have a trip tomorrow," she added.

She walked toward the guestroom where she was staying with a quick stride to avoid the conversation. "And what do you make of Israel?" the doctor asked as she made to open the door, knowing the bond between them since childhood.

She paused briefly, then shrugged at him. "He might be sick!" she mumbled and walked in, shutting the door behind her, with the couple staring after her

Chapter Nine

Mystery Unveil

Israel paced the room glumly. He had been like that since he came back from the agency. He couldn't believe all that he had heard today, though everything seemed to be making sense now. Upon getting to the agency, he saw the security guard he had met the other day.

"Hello," he greeted. The guard, named Moses, came around and stood before him. Israel had come to know his name after their brief conversation. "I hope you still remember me?" he asked, trying to see if the young man still recalled his face.

"Who wouldn't remember you," Moses replied. "Aren't you that queer guy from the other day? You came here, telling me you came with an invisible friend of yours. You even got me wondering if you were nuts or unwell that day," he said politely, trying not to use the word insane.

Israel had his hand to his chin briefly, remembering that Mayan had given him the same expression as Moses did that very day. "I'm sorry about that," he apologized. "However, I was just trying to do some finding, but I guess I'm okay now," he said. "So, what's the name?" he had asked.

Now, combining Mayan's story and that of this guard, he had come to believe that he was being haunted. But why? he kept asking himself while moving around the pace of Slim's living room. He wanted an answer, and he believed if Slim was haunting him, it must be for a reason. He was sure that his ghost resided inside the house.

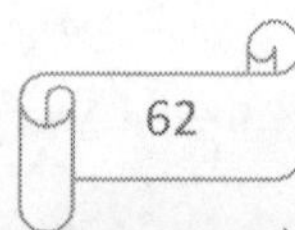

The whole setup seemed like a long nightmare to him. "Why Slim? Why did you come here?" he asked aloud.

He was quiet for a while, and then he spoke again. "Answer me, Slim!" he yelled out suddenly. "I know you are here. Oh! I forgot, your real name isn't Slim; you're Nickerson Miguel Eglin. So now answer me, please! Give me an answers I demand of you," he said, speaking to the lifeless room.

Suddenly, everything inside the house went dead for a moment, and there was lightning outside. The lights inside the house all went off and then came back on. They flickered for a while and finally went off again, leaving the living room in total darkness. More lightning struck outside. However, he sat calmly, not scared. He needed an answer to this mystical tale.

There was a whirlwind in the room, and all the pictures began to shatter. Several lightnings struck outside, and some hit heavily inside the house. His hair stood on end, but he stood still, determined to get an answer to this weird experience. He felt the presence of a being inside the house. However, he didn't intend to run; no, he wouldn't, because he wanted to get an answer to this enigma.

Then he saw it. Slim was sitting on his favorite couch, and the lightning made out his face. It was grotesque, a half-human flesh interwoven with worms and a half-decaying skull. His shirt looked shredded. Everything went blank again, and then the lightning came again, half-shining on him. This time, it had taken a form. He looked like the Slim Israel used to know. Israel moved toward him. "Why, Slim? Why are you haunting me? What do you want to tell me?" he asked anxiously.

However, Slim stood up and stared blankly at the room for a moment. He looked different now, rarely talking, looking serious and focused—a rare attitude from the Slim Israel usually knew. "Let's go for a walk," Slim said while holding Israel by the hand. Israel attempted to release his wrist from the grip, but he couldn't. He noticed they were gliding now. Moreover, they glided toward the wall.

“Where are we going?” Israel asked curiously, seeing they were not heading toward the door. Nick was more like a changed person, rarely saying a word. Israel shut his eyes as they approached the wall, fearing they were going to bang against it. He opened his eyes a few moments later, noticing nothing had happened.

“Where is this?” he asked. It appeared to be a big mansion. A woman was sitting in a corner in a big room by a big table, in a huge house. The house looked familiar to him. He was sure he had been here a long time ago. Now he recognized the house. He walked toward the woman and noticed she was holding a picture and sobbing quietly over it. He gazed at her and recognized the woman at once. She was Mrs. Miguel, Slim's mother, holding his picture and weeping over it.

“Oh, my son,” she said. “Why did you have to leave me this soon?” she lamented.

  He walked to her quietly. “Hi, Mrs. Miguel,” he managed to say. “Nick is here, ma'am. Stop weeping, please,” he said, trying to console her. He was surprised she was not even listening to him or seemed to be aware of his presence. She looked weak, old, and dull now. She wasn’t the same woman who used to inspire and motivate them those days. “Mrs. Miguel!” he called.

“She can't hear you! We are in a trance mode. We came here through teleportation,” Nick explained. “Right now, we are in a trance mode. You can see and touch, but no one sees you, except the people who are scarcely aware of your departure or know you by your real name, and also those you choose to see you. It is a temporary stage before you are completely transformed from the earth to the world of the celestial,” he explained further.

Israel turned to look at him with a quick frown. “Does that mean I am about to die as well?” he asked, feeling a little scared, especially after what had been happening to him in the last few days.

Slim turned his gaze to look at him and smiled. “No, you’re just in a state of trance where you are actually sitting right now in my room.

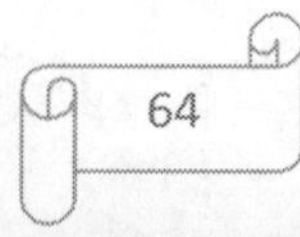

This is like an imaginary dream; the only difference is that it is real to you, because right now, you are in my world."

"So why did you bring me here?" he asked. "Your mum can't feel my presence. I would have tried consoling her in person. I have no use here, and she is bitter, all because of you."

Slim grimaced and watched her for a while. "She promised not to weep before my departure… but I knew that was not going to be possible. I'm her only male child, and me departing without an heir to her is like a big blow, really hurting and devastating," he explained, standing there white as snow, observing her.

"So where do I come in?" Israel asked. "You can't make her an heir again. Besides, it's a little or too late now," he pointed out.

"That's not for you to decide," Slim replied sharply. "Now, let's go." And in a moment, they appeared to be in another part of the world again. Israel marveled at the rate at which they traveled in just a few seconds. It was like every wall they went through led them to another country. A few minutes ago, he was in Mexico and now elsewhere. He was amazed at where they were now. A house, scantily decorated, looked a little dilapidated. It was a story building, which he could tell from the elevation of the window. Two young ladies sat, facing each other on a bed. He could swear by their accents that they were Brazilians.

"Who are those?" he asked, knowing perfectly well they couldn't see or hear them as well.

"Have you tried contacting his family since then?" Marissa asked, her voice trembling with concern. "I don't want to help you and then have them come here, suing us for aborting his baby. You know how those rich Mexicans can be, especially when it comes to a child."

"You know my dad, Marissa," the younger, more charming girl replied, her voice heavy with despair. "He's too religious and a fanatic as well. He won't tolerate me having a bastard under his roof.

He will kill me if he knows I'm pregnant. It's been just over a month now. I have to do something before it starts showing."

They both sat quietly for a moment, the weight of their situation settling over them like a dark cloud.

"Have you tried contacting his family?" Marissa asked again, her eyes searching her friend's face.

"I have tried," she whispered, her voice breaking. "We used to talk back then when he first left for Cuba. But after he went to Mexico to his family, he told me he wanted to go to the U.S. to get his documents for a law firm. And after that, I never heard from him again. I called later, and a lady answered..." She paused, her face contorting with a frown. "That's when I learned he was gone, Marissa. That's when I learned I had lost my Nick." She broke down, weeping uncontrollably.

Marissa hugged her friend passionately, her heart aching. "You should have introduced yourself," she murmured. "Perhaps he already told them about you. Let's not rush into this. This was his only memory, and I'm certain his family would hold you in high esteem for it."

"I can't do that, Marissa. I'm sure he never got the time to tell them. I only informed him about it the night before the incident. They told me he died on the way to the airport. They may think I'm a phony. I already gave it a shot, Marissa, but I can't bring myself to do it."

"Are you determined to go on with this plan? Is that right?" Marissa asked, her voice filled with concern. "You know there could be complications."

She sat thoughtfully for a brief moment, tears welling up in her eyes. "I've weighed it, and I don't think I have much of a choice. He had promised to come back and take me to his mother. He said she would love me. I thought he would come soon, but now he's dead. It's been over a month now, and I'm scared of my dad. I don't have a choice here, Marissa. My dad will kill me if he knew about it." She broke down once again, sobbing.

Marissa embraced her friend, her own tears falling. "I'm really sorry all this is happening to you. You're too young to be going through this. My only concern is your safety, and that's what I'm considering. But since you've made up your mind, we'll go there the day after tomorrow. The man isn't in town yet, but he said he'd be back by then."

Estella nodded, her resolve firm. "I'm ready to take the chance. I just hope you're sure it won't go wrong. I don't want to lose the baby or myself in the process."

Marissa grimaced and heaved a sigh. "That, I can't guarantee, my friend. But I've heard a lot about him. They say he's good at what he does. Don't worry, I wouldn't take you there if I hadn't tried him myself." She assured her affirmatively.

The two girls were quiet again; Israel and Nick watched them for some moments in their trance mode. "So that was the girl you told me about when you were in Brazil, right?" Israel asked. "Well, she is really cute," he complimented.

"Yes, she is," Nick replied coldly. "About a month and some weeks back after I left Santa Clara, I got an offer to start a law firm in New York. Sorry I never told you about it," he said apologetically. "I wanted to make it a surprise. I was overwhelmed with joy on the night of the offer, and as I was getting set to go, I got a call with good news. And I was the happiest man that night, because I would be getting a license for a law firm and at the same time going to be a dad with a girl I am very much in love with. Though I planned on telling Mother and Mayan when I returned from my trip, that morning..." He stopped abruptly, his face showing a sudden sad expression. He looked sober for a while. "Mother gave me a king treatment that morning," he said. "She never knew it would be the last. I and Mr. Igor, the driver, drove to the airport. I asked to drive because Mother was scared of Mr. Igor's driving, as he often drove rough most of the time. Unknown to me, that my days were numbered. We got hit by a speeding truck, and instantly something

Israel watched him with amazement. "And what happened?" he asked curiously.

Slim stood undecided for a while and then continued. "I noticed I was outside the car, and my shirt was stained with blood. I walked back to the car to examine it, and I noticed Mr. Igor was still in the car, and a man was sitting at the wheel. They were both badly injured and unconscious. I tried to rush in and help out, but I noticed I couldn't touch the car because my hand was transparent. People rushed to the scene and brought out Mr. Igor and the person at the steering wheel. I moved closer to observe them closely, and that was when I got the biggest shock of my life, because I noticed the man on the steering wheel was me, and I was injured beyond recognition."

He was quiet again for a moment with a blank expression on his face. "I tried calling to the people because I didn't know what was happening to me, but my body was carried to the hospital along with that of the driver. I tried getting back to my skin, but something kept pushing me away and preventing me. My mother later came in, along with Mayan, and they both wept, and I watched them weeping sadly." He explained and paused again. "And suddenly, I was back to my body again. However, I knew I only had a few minutes because I never fully fit back. But in those few moments, I noticed I could appear wherever I wanted to, and I also noticed I could be seen by people who aren't my blood relatives and those who don't call me by my real name. I learned a lot within seconds. I knew I needed help, and only one person I knew could fix that. I guess now you know the rest of the story," he concluded.

Israel nodded casually at him. "Now I know why you had chosen me," he said.

He suddenly realized that they were back at Slim's place, and Slim continued to narrate what happened. "I promised my mama I would tell her about it, but I never got the chance to do that. I only succeeded in making her promise that she would take her when she comes, and that was my last wish," he said.

"Did she know who you're referring to, and did she accept to take her?" Israel asked.

"Yes, she did promise to take her. It was my dying wish, so I guess you know where you come in now and also know what you must do, right?" he asked. Israel nodded to him in affirmation.

"You have to leave by dawn. I will give her a sign if she doubts you because I feel like I'm fading away, and I'm so certain that I don't have much time here anymore, and I would soon fade permanently." He explained and went quiet again. "Okay, I got to go catch some sights. Now try getting some sleep," he advised.

Israel shrugged at him. "Okay," he said and paused briefly. "One more thing," he said with a grin. "Now that I know everything, I hope I'm no longer in the trance or teleportation thing again. Right?" he asked, as now he was no longer scared of Slim/Nick; after all, he was his best friend.

They both laughed at his joke, and Israel woke up abruptly. Now he was all alone again, and the room became cool as it was when he had come in that evening, quiet again and silent as a graveyard. He stood up and walked out of the house, bolting the door from behind as he left.

Chapter Ten

Somewhere in Rio, Brazil

Israel walked the streets of Rio de Janeiro gallantly. It was a beautiful city, and he loved adventure. He wished he were here for fun. Now he understood why Slim had told him they never have all the time. He had taken a morning flight to Brazil, and from the airport, he had taken a taxi to the address Slim had given him. As he got closer to the house, he saw the two girls he had seen in his trance mode, and they were about to take a cab.

He hurried to them, as Marissa had already jumped into the back seat of the cab. "Excuse me, ladies. You must be Estella," he said while holding out his hand to her.

"Yes, of course," she replied with a little frown on her face. She was surprised at this stranger whom she knew she had never met before. "And who are you?" she asked curiously.

"I'm Israel Cruz. I came from Cuba, and I came here to see…"

"Sorry, Mr. Cruz," she cut in, leaving him mid-speech before he could finish what he was saying. "I'm having an important appointment now, and my friend here is taking me there. I suggest you come back later, and excuse me for now if you don't mind. Maybe we can see each other some other time," she said, simultaneously making an effort to join Marissa in the cab.

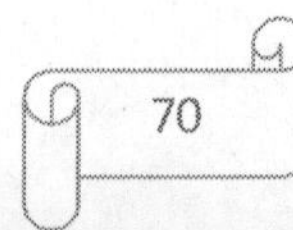

Israel grinned at her briefly. "I believe I'm here for the same reason," he said with some confidence, and this got her attention. She hadn't discussed this with anyone except Marissa, who looked astonished as well.

She turned to face Israel with genuine interest, and the cab driver began to honk, as he was already getting impatient with the ladies. "Where do you say you are from again? And what do you know about my appointment?" she asked curiously.

"Nice house you've got there!" he complimented. She knew it wasn't true and that he was only complimenting her in anticipation of getting her attention. The cab driver honked again and started saying something rashly in Spanish. "I guess we should go somewhere to talk this out. I wouldn't like your dad to see a stranger around his daughter, as I wouldn't want to get you in trouble," he said.

She knew he was right about her dad and she remembered what it took before Nick could win his admiration.

"Come on now, Estella! Let's go!" Marissa yelled at her from inside the cab. "We got business to do. Let the gentleman wait if he must see you. I got things to do. Besides, Santana will be waiting for us already," she added.

"Hi Marissa," Israel said, interrupting her even before she finished what she was saying. She paused and studied him for a while, wondering how he had come to know her name.

"And who is this guy?" she asked curiously. Estella shrugged at her friend in response.

"Get inside," Israel said to Estella. He went to the front seat and sat next to the driver. "And please ask him to take us to any nice restaurant here. I'm really famished," he said. Turning his gaze to Marissa, he added, "Marissa, please call the doctor and tell him you can't make it again."

"Why should I do that?" she asked with an angry tone. "Besides, the appointment is between him and my friend here, Estella! And I don't see your side of involvement," she said and paused abruptly, gazing hard at Estella for a moment. "Or did you invite him here?" she asked while staring inquisitively at her.

"No, I never invited him," Estella retorted sharply. "I don't even know or have ever seen him before, not until now. But he seems so confident of himself," she added.

"Well, ladies, let me shock you," Israel said with a grin. "She will die if you take her to the doctor. I'm here to help out, so I suggest you both do as I say and hear me out first, instead of all this melodrama."

The girls stared at each other briefly. Estella was quiet for a moment, then she told the driver a name, and Marissa made the call.

Some minutes later, they sat in an exotic restaurant with nice delicacies. The drinks were good, and there were many foreigners inside as well. The atmosphere was cozy, except for the bewildered expression that engulfed the faces of both Estella and Marissa, for they had hardly touched any of the expensive food or drinks Israel had ordered for them.

Estella and Marissa sat in dismay because everything Israel had said was true, and they had no choice but to believe him.

She was quiet for a while, then she asked, "But how do I convince my dad? He won't allow me to go. He doesn't even know that I am pregnant in the first place, and I don't want to break his heart," she said. She stopped again, then asked, "But why didn't he appear to me? He knows I missed him much. He could have at least appeared to me and explained himself."

"Well, I can't tell why myself because even I never knew he had departed, not until his sister came around and started giving me all sorts of weird gazes whenever I spoke about him to her."

She gestured at him and asked, "Is he here now?" She asked while looking inquisitively at Israel.

"No, he is not here. He had already completed his cycles, but he might appear again, though I'm not pretty sure about that," he added.

"So, back to the question, what do I tell my dad?" she asked again. "I quite certain that he won't just allow me travel out without knowing where I am going. I have to have a story."

Israel was quiet for a few minutes, as this was a puzzle he had not thought about before now. He sat quietly working on a plan in his head, as this was his best friend's wish, even though he now knew that Slim was dead and that he had been haunted by him before. However, he must help keep his memory alive. He smiled and finally brightened up. "I got an idea," he finally said.

Estella and Marissa stared at him in surprise. However, he smiled casually at them. "Mrs. Miguel will be expecting us soon," he said. "So eat up, girls, and let's start going. It's getting dark already," he pointed out.

Chapter Eleven

Mexico, Mrs. Miguel's Mansion

Mrs. Miguel sat by the chimney, going through some of the documents Mayan had brought back from Cuba. She studied them for a while, then remained quiet for a brief moment. All this stuff is just a memory now, she thought within herself. Well, she still had a daughter; she consoled herself and wiped the tears from her face.

Mayan walked into the big living room to join her mother. She had arrived the previous evening and had just taken a shower.

She observed her mother for a while and walked up to her. "Mom! Are you still going over that stuff again? Don't overwork yourself, Mama. It has been a month now. Don't start by giving yourself a heart problem," she said and walked over to her mother, sitting by her side.

Hand in hand, mother and daughter sat quietly. They sat so for some minutes.

"How is Cuba?" Mrs. Miguel asked, breaking the icy silence. "I am sure Robert and his wife are doing well, right?"

"Yes, Mama. They are both good," she replied. "And they sent their regards. They are really a nice couple. Though I would have loved to stay back there for a while, but every day I spent there kept bringing me memories of him and Dad. However, they are gone now."

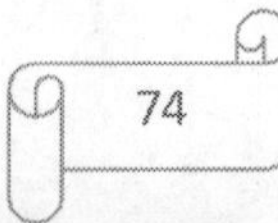

They both sighed at her remarks. "So how is Israel? Did you see him? Did he tell you why he never came to pay condolences for your brother? Of all the people I could think of, he was the least I could imagine being absent, even though they were best friends and were more like brothers," she noted and stopped abruptly, observing Mayan who looked a little absent-minded. "Are you okay, baby?" she asked.

She paused, then shrugged at her mother. "Mama! You don't want to hear this part," she said. "It's just so annoying and astonishing that I can't even tell who to believe or what to believe," she added.

Mrs. Miguel sat up and stared at her daughter curiously. "What is it, my baby? What are you not telling me?" she asked calmly. "I hope you don't mean to tell me Israel never knew your brother is late? Because that will be the biggest lie I have ever heard."

"I wish that was it, Mama! But it's even more terrible than that," she retorted. At that point, Mrs. Miguel adjusted her seat, facing her, wondering what her daughter found so absurd and hard to discuss.

"I saw him twice," she started to say, "and both times, he was acting queer. He kept acting weird and doing creepy things. Like the first time we met, he came with his car and greeted me. Then all of a sudden, he started asking an imaginary Nick to join him because they had somewhere to go." She laughed to herself at the thought of the event. "He even opened his car door for the imaginary Nick and drove away, telling me they would be back as he drove off." She stopped and observed her mother for a moment, then continued. "And on the second occasion, I had to put him in his place. I got so fed up with his nonsense that I had to shut him up," she said.

Elizabeth was quiet for a while, a lot of thoughts running through her head. She knew Israel was her daughter's first and only crush since childhood, and she perceived Mayan couldn't be making this up for any reason. "So he didn't believe Nick was dead? And he told you Nick was in Cuba all this while?" she asked calmly.

"Mama! Please stop making anything out of this. You see why I never want to talk about this in the first place?" she asked and paused briefly. "There is a lot of ghost talk in Santa Clara lately. He might have gotten one of those ideas into his head and believed he was still seeing Nick. However, as far as we are both concerned, Mama, we both know Nick died and we buried him. So don't let us bring back sad memories now," she said.

Her mother, however, was quiet for a brief moment, a lot of thoughts running through her mind. "I know that, baby," she finally said. "But sometimes a lot of mystics happen. You should have given him a chance to clear himself. I know as a medical practitioner and a conventional person, you will find it hard to believe those talks. But sometimes, we cannot underestimate or comprehend the fact behind supernatural manifestations," she explained.

"Mother! Please stop now! Can we just pretend we never had this conversation? Please, Mother, don't you think I respect Israel too? He is my brother's best friend and even my closest friend as well. And I know he is like a son to you too. However, I can't let anyone bring back that sad memory again. Please, Mama, let's not talk…"

She stopped mid-speech as Claudia, their housemaid, came in, thereby interrupting her. "I am sorry to bother you, Madam, but a gentleman and a young lady are here to see you," she said. "He said his name is Israel, and he is a distant relative of yours."

Mrs. Miguel and her daughter stood speechless for a brief moment, staring at each other in amazement.

"Should I let them in, Ma'am?" Claudia asked.

"Oh! Hurry, let them in quickly," she said after regaining her breath. "He is my other son," she added.

Mayan stood there amazed. She was speechless and wondered what this sudden visit was all about now.

A few minutes later, Israel sat on one of the big couches inside the big living room. It had been almost two years since the last time he visited this place, and that was when Nick's family had first moved back home. He remembered the adventures with Nick around the town; however, everything was quiet now. Estella also sat on one of the two-seater sofas, looking a little tense and nervous, especially as she perceived Mayan was constantly inspecting her since the time she walked into the house. Although it wasn't a hostile look, she wondered what the inspection was about.

 Mrs. Miguel and her daughter sat on the big three-seater sofa facing Israel, who seemed to be enjoying his coffee and really felt at home. She liked the boy a lot, and she saw him as one of her own. He had grown up with them back then in Cuba and had always been like a son to her. He often stayed much in their home then, and even his own mother used to be jealous of how her biological son fancied Slim's mother rather than his own home. His presence had almost made her forget the issue on the ground.

"Wow! What a surprising visit!" Mayan said, breaking the silence. "You never told me that you would be coming here the last time we saw each other. Though I know I was mad at you then," she admitted with a smile, "but you sure deserved it."

Israel took a sip from his drink and turned to her. "Well, that was that," he said, then turned to her mother. "Accept my deep condolences, Mrs. Miguel. I'm truly sorry I never came in time," he noted apologetically. "But seriously, I still can't believe that he is really gone even now. And as for the visit," he said after a brief pause, "I never planned it, and it came to me unprepared that I don't even know where to start from," he said, while observing Mayan and her mother.

"I understand," Elizabeth chipped in mildly. "Mayan and I were just talking about you, and I was surprised when Claudia came in and asked to let you in. What a coincidence?" she said.

He dropped his cup on a mini table at his side and grimaced briefly. "Well, let me start by introducing this young lady here," he said.

"She is Estella, and she is from Rio in Brazil. It took me all the courage in this world to get her here. I even had to lie to her father that she was offered a year scholarship here. However, your decision after here will determine her fate," he added.

He stopped briefly, noticing Mayan inspecting Estella closely now.

"I think I remember where I have seen her now," Mayan said curtly, standing to her feet and walking closer to Estella, who was already feeling a little uneasy. "I think she was that girl in Nick's phone. He had her on his displayed background picture of his phone. Don't you remember, Mama?" she asked.

Mrs. Miguel shrugged at her. "I can't really recall every girl's picture in my late son's phone," she said. "Besides, the phone was destroyed in the accident," she pointed out. At her remark, a loop of tears dropped from Estella's eyes. "So where do we come in?" she asked Israel curiously.

Israel rubbed his hands for a while, as he was unsure of where to begin. However, he cleared his throat and began. "First of all, I came to fix up some puzzles, which I only hope that you would take your time to hear me out," he muttered briefly and paused for a moment again. "Two days ago, you were inside your room by the mirror, holding Nick's picture and weeping over it. I hope you remember that," he asked.

Mrs. Miguel's face brightened up suddenly. She had known this boy since he was a kid, and he was never a creepy boy in all those times. But now, he mystified her a little with his riddles. "I was all alone, and nobody would have known that," she said in a surprised gesture.

"You remember on the day of the incident, he had said that he wanted to tell you something, but he'd promised he would do that when he returned from his trip, and that which he never did. I'm sure you do remember that as well?" he asked.

Mayan stared at her mother for a brief moment. She would have stopped him, but they both remembered the event vividly, and all he had said so far was true.

He studied them both for a moment, and then he went on. "Before his last breath, he asked you to do him a favor, which you didn't actually understand what he meant. However, you had accepted that you would do it and take her if she ever comes. I'm sure you recall that too?" he asked again.

Mrs. Miguel recalled all those moments. It was a horrible experience. She remembered that fateful day and all that had happened. "How did you come to know all that?" she asked soberly, and a tear began to drop down her cheek. Mayan walked to her mother and started consoling her.

"It's okay now, Israel!" she said. "You see what you've caused her now? You are bringing back those memories again," she quarreled, and she noticed Estella was sobbing as well.

"I'm sorry, Mayan," he apologized. "I'm not comfortable doing this either. Besides, I never wanted to do any of this. From the start, I never knew he was late, and I swear to you, it hurt me to be the one he had to choose for this. However, I just want to get over with this haunting by my best friend," he said.

He paused now while gazing at Mrs. Miguel, who seemed a little uncertain if she wanted him to stop, but from her expression, he could tell that she wanted to hear it all.

"I can stop now, Mrs. Miguel, however, if that's what you want. Though he asked me to come, but if it hurts you as much as I can see it does, I can hold on and continue when you're strong enough to take it again," he said.

"It's okay now," Mayan retorted sharply. "She won't have any more of this. Besides, can't you see you are causing her much hurt already? Please stop."

"No, Israel! I want to hear it all," Mrs. Miguel interjected. "At least I have taken it this far, and from all the points you have made, there is much element of truth in all that you have said. So let us hear it all and get over with it.

"Mother!" Mayan yelled, "are you sure you want to do this?" she asked.

"I just said so, Mayan!" she retorted firmly while wiping the tears from her eyes. "Now, go on, Israel," she said while nodding at him in approval.

Israel sat relaxed and stared at her with relief. "Well, as I was saying," he started, and he narrated everything to Mrs. Miguel, starting from when Slim had returned to the West End, to how he had found Estella, and why he was finally there. "So that was it, Mrs. Miguel. Now I feel relieved," he said, heaving a deep sigh.

Mayan and her mother sat still for a while. The house was quiet for a brief moment, while Israel observed them quietly, wondering if they still thought him to be insane.

However, Mrs. Miguel stood up and walked up to Estella. She studied her for a brief moment. The young lady felt a little uneasy, especially at the way she was being scrutinized. Mrs. Miguel lowered herself and sat closer to Estella, holding her hands in an assured gesture to make her feel at ease.

"So how old is it?" she asked while staring at the young lady's tummy. Estella felt a little shy at her question. She was only raised by her father because she had lost her mother when she was still a toddler. Aside from that, she was not accustomed to motherly nurture.

"A month and some weeks plus now, Ma," she replied softly, feeling rather shy. Although she felt uncomfortable with Mrs. Miguel at first, her calmness gave her some motherly comfort.

"So he only knew about it a night before the accident?" she asked. Israel nodded in reply. Mrs. Miguel admired Estella briefly. Now she understood everything. This was what he had promised to tell her when he got back from the trip that morning. However, he never knew life was too short. Either way, she was glad Israel had gone this far even for a late friend, even though it was a mystic she couldn't unveil. However, she couldn't deny the fact that he had really fixed the missing part of the puzzle just as he had said.

"Well, I will make arrangements to contact your dad," she said while caressing Estella's beautiful hair. "We have to let him know the situation on the ground. I am really glad you came. You don't know how happy I felt, to know that my only son left me an heir, even after I thought all was lost except for Mayan."

"No, please!" Estella pleaded. "He never knew I was pregnant. He is a very religious man, and he holds me in high esteem, and it will break his heart. I only pray you do me this favor and stick to Israel's initial plan that I was on a scholarship. I think that will not hurt him much," she pleaded

Mayan gazed at her mother briefly. She knew how strict she was, but the joy of her late son having a child was too great news for her. She would do anything to keep Nick's name alive, even bending her rules.

"Scholarship?" she asked while smiling. "So Israel came up with that idea to get you here? I see you have turned into a great inventor of lies now, Israel," she said jokingly. "But certainly! Scholarship she wants, and scholarship she must have. Now let us all go, get something to eat, and celebrate this great news. And as for you, Estella, you're going to live a life of a queen here, more than you could ever have imagined," she said while pulling Estella by her hand and walking her to the big dining table.

Mayan watched her mother with joy as she walked her new daughter to the table. It had been a while since she had seen her looking this happy, and it gave her joy to see life in her again.

"I guess you'll be staying till the weekend?" she asked, turning to Israel who was stretching and getting ready to join Mrs. Miguel at the table.

"I will be leaving by tomorrow. I got a lot to do. Moreover, I had only come to keep my part of the agreement, which I am glad I did," he said and stopped abruptly with a grimace. "I still can't believe that he is truly gone. Well, you will have to take me to his grave later. I would like to go pay my last respects," he added.

She studied him for a moment, wondering how he had felt after knowing he was being haunted and still carried out such a weird assignment that had taken courage to attain. "Do you still see him?" she asked anxiously.

Israel turned his gaze to her and smiled. "No, not after the teleportation and the transient thing. Perhaps he might appear again to say his final goodbye," he replied.

"I am sure you must have felt deceived, especially as you are not the only one that had seen him, and yet I was always doubting you, right?" she asked.

He shrugged at her. "Well, I was, at the time," he said. "But later I got used to it. He was my best friend, a brother I never had. Who else would he have entrusted with such a weird mission? I'm sure not even you, his sister," he added.

She grinned at him with a gesture. "I could not have been able to handle it," she said. "And I'm quite sure that if it was me, by now I would have been in a psychiatrist's home. I have heard many ghost stories; I never knew I would be having one in my family and even with a living proof."

He smiled and patted her shoulder passionately. "I am glad he chose me. I would still do it for him again and again if he still had more missions. However, I am glad it has finally come to an end. Now, let's go and eat. I am damn famished," he said, standing up.

She smiled at him, and he held out his hand to her and pulled her up. They both walked, holding hands, to the dining table to join Mrs. Miguel and Estella, who sat patiently waiting for them.

Chapter Twelve

Final Enigma

Troy sat on a big couch in his dimly lit living room, the flickering glow from the TV casting long shadows on the walls. He had just bid his little sister Jessica goodnight. For a while now, he had not seen Slim or Israel around. He felt at ease with himself, especially considering all that had happened lately—events that had both amazed and mystified him. However, he couldn't relate any of it to Israel, especially since he and Slim were best friends and fancied each other a lot. He decided to keep everything to himself.

He sat quietly, watching an action movie, when suddenly he heard an owl hoot outside. His hair stood on end. "What a bad omen?" he thought to himself. He hated the sound made by owls or cats. And as he stood still, he heard sudden movement in his basement. "What is that again?" he mumbled to himself. He stood up and walked down to the basement to see what it was; he had just cleaned up the basement today and was certain that there were no rats around the house.

He got down to the basement and picked up a flashlight. He checked around for a while but found nothing. However, he kept looking around to make sure there was nothing there. He was certain he had heard a noise from down here. "Okay, there is nothing here," he muttered to himself with satisfaction.

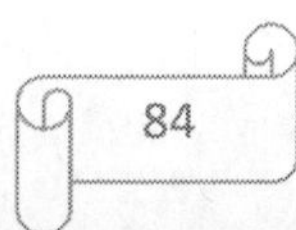

After making sure everything was okay, he walked up the stairs to his living room again. Just as he was about to sit down, he heard another sound coming from the kitchen. "What is it now?" he asked himself. He rushed to see what was there and got there just in time to see it leaving.

It was a big cat, and he wondered how it had gotten in. He never liked cats, due to his superstitious beliefs, especially after the lecture he received from Slim and what had happened to his sister the other night.

"Hey, Catty, how did you get in?" he asked. He stopped and smiled to himself; he couldn't believe he was talking to a strange animal, even though he knew it couldn't talk back. "Well, you've got to go out now, Catty," he said. He walked to the kitchen's exit door and opened it to let the cat out.

The animal stared at him for a moment before walking out and stopping just outside the exit door. He closed the glass door behind him, satisfied that he had let the cat out. However, he was surprised that the cat just sat outside and didn't leave his doorstep. For all he cared, this was the least of his worries. All that mattered now was that he had let the animal out. He shut the glass door, and as he was about to leave, he turned to look at the cat. Their eyes met, and there was a dazzling reflection in its eyes. It scared him so much that he quickly walked back toward his living room. Just then, an owl hooted again, scaring him so much that he almost burst into a trot in his own house.

"Oh God, what is this omen?" he asked himself in a frightened gesture. "A cat, an owl? What a very weird night…" he began to say before suddenly halting.

"You look really terrible, buddy… I could swear you look like someone who had just met with the devil himself. Come on, what is chasing you, buddy?" asked an unmistakable voice.

He almost fainted at the sound of the voice. He hasn't expected anyone to be in his living room at this hour of the night. Besides, he was certain he had bolted the entrance doors just some minutes earlier. He stood there, white and speechless.

*** ** ***

Israel was busy packing his things with Mayan helping him. Her mother had packed some of Nick's stuff for him, saying she was certain Nick would have wanted him to have them. She had kept the rest for the unborn child, so he/she would have something as a souvenir when they grew up.

"You'll be home this time tomorrow," Mayan said with a sad expression on her face. She looked a little sad, perceiving she would be all by herself again by the morrow. His presence had brightened and gladdened her, reminding her of the good times they used to share back in Cuba as a big family. She couldn't help but feel she was already missing him. However, thanks to him, she now had someone as a sister; Estella would fill the gap and keep her company now.

Her mother had made arrangements with the Mexico Science University, and with her prestige, they had agreed to enroll Estella in a two-year medical course after some assessment. She had also called her father to let him know that she was okay, which was a good thing for all of them.

Israel watched Mayan admiringly for a brief moment and smiled at her. She looked cute and adorable in her native attire as she helped him pack up.

"Come on, Mayan! It's not like I'll be gone forever," he said. "Besides, I'll be coming back to check on you guys more often from now on," he promised, "and especially on you!" he added emphatically.

They stared at each other for a brief moment, and then she giggled and smiled at him. Her family seemed to be happy again, and her mother was just too fond of Estella, treating her like a dear daughter. Maybe it was because she was carrying her grandchild or for the

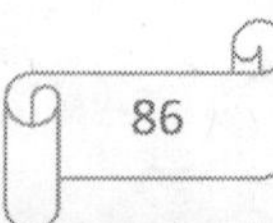

sake of Nick's memory. Regardless, anyone would have loved this girl for no reason other than her sweet and humble nature, despite her beauty. She wasn't surprised at how her brother had easily fallen in love with her.

She wished he were alive; it would have been the best family ever. "What are your plans?" she asked suddenly while helping him pack. "It's been a while since we last talked about you," she noted.

He shrugged with a grin. "Well, it's still the usual thing. Though the stock market isn't moving smoothly lately, I'm working on starting my own outsourcing business. What do you make of that?" he asked.

"It isn't a bad idea. Just be sure you have your mind made up about it first," she advised.

"That is nice of you, and I think you would make a good personal assistant," he joked. They both laughed loudly. At that moment, his phone began to ring. He quickly took it out of his pocket, checked the caller, glanced briefly at her, and then answered the call.

"Hey, Troy! What's up with you? Well, good timing you called me. What's happening around…"

"You don't believe what I told you the other time, right? Now I am certain that my guess is right," Troy said, speaking rashly and cutting him off before he could finish speaking.

"Hey, hey, hey! What's biting you?" he asked in a calm tone. "You seem to be excited and all worked up. Calm down and take it one step at a time. It's midnight, right? So what are you still doing up this late?" he asked.

"Listen," Troy retorted while explaining his shock to Israel, who stood quietly listening on the other end. Mayan watched him closely. She knew it had something to do with her brother, but she couldn't tell what it was about this time, especially since it was from Troy.

Troy spoke rashly for a while, with Israel quietly listening all the while. "Are you still there, man? You don't seem to believe me, though I already knew you wouldn't. I just needed to talk to someone," he said.

Israel was silent for a moment and then spoke. "I believe you, buddy! I believe you," he said and paused. "However, I don't see it the way you pointed out," he replied.

"You believe me?" he asked in a surprised tone. "Wow! First time you are with me on this issue. So what do you think of it? Because right now, I'm really freaking out, and I can't seem to get hold of myself or get the event out of my head," he added emphatically.

Israel sighed briefly, contemplating where to start, and then he spoke again. "So he came to tell you that he would be gone for a long, long time and that he was only there to let you know because he couldn't leave without saying goodbye to you. Is that right?" he asked.

"Yes, that's what he said. He walked out of the house, leaving me in a frozen state. By the time I regained my breath, he was already out of the house. I rushed out to say bye, but I didn't see him. I didn't hear his car leave, and he couldn't have gone far. I'm certain I couldn't have missed him," he replied.

Israel stood speechless for a while, thinking of what to say in response. "Perhaps you were so frightened that you didn't notice when he drove off because I'm quite sure he couldn't have just vanished into thin air, as you said."

"I know what I saw," he retorted sharply. "I was just a couple of steps behind him. It all happened so quickly, and I swear to you, it was all mystical. I couldn't have missed him," he said, stopping for a moment. "Where are you now? Because I checked on you during the day, and your place was locked up. A neighbor told me you weren't in town! You never told me you would be traveling," he said and paused briefly. "You guys have been acting queer lately," he noted.

Israel stared at Mayan and grinned. "I'm in Mexico," he said. "I'm at Slim's place. I came yesterday because Slim sent me on an errand."

There was a long pause before Troy spoke again. "You're in Mexico? Hmmm…" he mumbled from the other end. "And you never bothered to let me know?" he asked, a hint of disappointment in his voice, followed by a deep sigh.

"Get some rest, buddy!" He replied mildly, "Moreover, I'll be back by tomorrow. We have a lot to talk about. Besides, I believe you got a long night to clear off your head from your dreadful experience, so get some sleep," Israel advised, trying to sound soothing.

There was another long silence. Finally, Troy heaved a sigh from the other end. "Goodnight," he replied coldly. "Send my regards to Mayan and her mama," he said, and the line went dead.

"Nick, I guess, paying some visit to Troy, right?" Mayan asked, concern etched on her face.

"You guessed right. He just visited him and vanished. He told him he would be gone for a long time. However, he will be shocked to know the actual truth by tomorrow," Israel said, trying to mask his own unease.

"Of course, he would be. But why doesn't he appear to us, his family? I mean, me and mama? What I wouldn't give just to see him for a moment," she said, her voice trembling with longing.

"He's done that already," Israel retorted gently. "He came back for that at the hospital, remember?" She nodded in affirmation, tears welling up in her eyes. "Now go get some sleep," he advised. "It's late already."

She giggled softly, trying to lift her spirits, and stood to her feet. "I will do just that," she said, leaning over him and planting a passionate kiss on his cheek with a bright smile on her face. "Thanks, Israel!" she said. "And that's for everything you've done for us." She turned and walked to her room, leaving him gazing after her speechlessly.

"You are welcome," he finally replied faintly, regaining his breath after a split second.

Mrs. Miguel watched them from a keyhole in her door. "Thanks, Nick!" she mumbled softly. "You didn't only bring me a grandchild, but you have also made me a family." She walked back quietly to her big bed, a tear of gratitude slipping down her cheek.

Israel walked to his room and sat on the bed. It was Nick's room. He sat by the edge of the bed, reminiscing about the time they had spent together when he had first come here. He turned and lay down, gazing at Nick's picture, which still sat on the table beside the lamp stand by his bedside.

Suddenly, there was a strong whirlwind howling and rattling inside the room. The curtains flew in the air, and there was a rattling noise all over the room for a while. The picture on the table fell face down, and finally, everything went quiet and back to normal.

He smiled within himself. "Hello, Slim," he said. "Oh! I forgot. It's Nick I meant to say. Either way, it's you. I know you are here to say goodbye. And I through I can't see you, but I can still feel your presence. I am going to miss you a lot... However, goodbye for now, my brother and friend." He fell back on the big bed, feeling extremely exhausted, and slept off.

The End

Made in the USA
Monee, IL
08 July 2026

56550075R00052